MASSIMILLA DONI

HONORE DE BALZAC

Translated by Clara Bell and James Waring

Massimilla Doni

Honore de Balzac

© 1st World Library – Literary Society, 2005
PO Box 2211
Fairfield, IA 52556
www.1stworldlibrary.org
First Edition

LCCN: 2005906493

Softcover ISBN: 1-4218-1549-4
Hardcover ISBN: 1-4218-1449-8
eBook ISBN: 1-4218-1649-0

Purchase *"Massimilla Doni"*
as a traditional bound book at:
www.1stWorldLibrary.org/purchase.asp?ISBN=1-4218-1549-4

1st World Library Literary Society is a nonprofit
organization dedicated to promoting literacy by:

- Creating a free internet library accessible from any
  computer worldwide.
- Hosting writing competitions and offering book
  publishing scholarships.

Massimilla Doni
contributed by Tim, Ed & Rodney
in support of
1st World Library Literary Society

DEDICATION

To Jacques Strunz.

MY DEAR STRUNZ: - I should be ungrateful if I did not set your name at the head of one of the two tales I could never have written but for your patient kindness and care. Accept this as my grateful acknowledgment of the readiness with which you tried - perhaps not very successfully - to initiate me into the mysteries of musical knowledge. You have at least taught me what difficulties and what labor genius must bury in those poems which procure us transcendental pleasures. You have also afforded me the satisfaction of laughing more than once at the expense of a self-styled connoisseur.

Some have taxed me with ignorance, not knowing that I have taken counsel of one of our best musical critics, and had the benefit of your conscientious help. I have, perhaps, been an inaccurate amanuensis. If this were the case, I should be the traitorous translator without knowing it, and I yet hope to sign myself always one of your friends.

DE BALZAC.

MASSIMILLA DONI

As all who are learned in such matters know, the Venetian aristocracy is the first in Europe. Its *Libro d'Oro* dates from before the Crusades, from a time when Venice, a survivor of Imperial and Christian Rome which had flung itself into the waters to escape the Barbarians, was already powerful and illustrious, and the head of the political and commercial world.

With a few rare exceptions this brilliant nobility has fallen into utter ruin. Among the gondoliers who serve the English - to whom history here reads the lesson of their future fate - there are descendants of long dead Doges whose names are older than those of sovereigns. On some bridge, as you glide past it, if you are ever in Venice, you may admire some lovely girl in rags, a poor child belonging, perhaps, to one of the most famous patrician families. When a nation of kings has fallen so low, naturally some curious characters will be met with. It is not surprising that sparks should flash out among the ashes.

These reflections, intended to justify the singularity of the persons who figure in this narrative, shall not be indulged in any longer, for there is nothing more intolerable than the stale reminiscences of those who insist on talking about Venice after so many great poets and petty travelers. The interest of the tale requires only this record of the most startling contrast in the life of man: the dignity and poverty which are conspicuous there in some of the men as they are in most of the houses.

The nobles of Venice and of Geneva, like those of Poland in former times, bore no titles. To be named Quirini, Doria, Brignole, Morosini, Sauli, Mocenigo, Fieschi, Cornaro, or Spinola, was enough for the pride of the haughtiest. But all things become corrupt. At the present day some of these families have titles.

And even at a time when the nobles of the aristocratic republics were all equal, the title of Prince was, in fact, given at Genoa to a member of the Doria family, who were sovereigns of the principality of Amalfi, and a similar title was in use at Venice, justified by ancient inheritance from Facino Cane, Prince of Varese. The Grimaldi, who assumed sovereignty, did not take possession of Monaco till much later.

The last Cane of the elder branch vanished from Venice thirty years before the fall of the Republic, condemned for various crimes more or less criminal. The branch on whom this nominal principality then devolved, the Cane Memmi, sank into poverty during the fatal period between 1796 and 1814. In the twentieth year of the present century they were represented only by a young man whose name was Emilio, and an old palace which is regarded as one of the chief ornaments of the Grand Canal. This son of Venice the Fair had for his whole fortune this useless Palazzo, and fifteen hundred francs a year derived from a country house on the Brenta, the last plot of the lands his family had formerly owned on *terra firma*, and sold to the Austrian government. This little income spared our handsome Emilio the ignominy of accepting, as many nobles did, the indemnity of a franc a day, due to every impoverished patrician under the stipulations of the cession to Austria.

At the beginning of winter, this young gentleman was still lingering in a country house situated at the base of the Tyrolese Alps, and purchased in the previous spring by the Duchess Cataneo. The house, erected by Palladio for the Piepolo family, is a square building of the finest style of architecture. There is a stately staircase with a marble portico on each side; the vestibules are crowded with frescoes, and made light by sky-blue ceilings across which graceful figures float amid ornament rich in design, but so well proportioned that the building carries it, as a woman carries her head-dress, with an ease that charms the eye; in short, the grace and dignity that characterize the *Procuratie* in the piazetta at Venice. Stone walls, admirably decorated, keep the rooms at a pleasantly cool temperature. Verandas outside, painted in fresco, screen off the glare. The flooring throughout is the old Venetian inlay of marbles, cut into unfading flowers.

The furniture, like that of all Italian palaces, was rich with handsome silks, judiciously employed, and valuable pictures favorably hung; some by the Genoese priest, known as *il Capucino*, several by Leonardo da Vinci, Carlo Dolci, Tintoretto, and Titian.

The shelving gardens were full of the marvels where money has been turned into rocky grottoes and patterns of shells, - the very madness of craftsmanship, - terraces laid out by the fairies, arbors of sterner aspect, where the cypress on its tall trunk, the triangular pines, and the melancholy olive mingled pleasingly with orange trees, bays, and myrtles, and clear pools in which blue or russet fishes swam. Whatever may be said in favor of the natural or English garden, these trees, pruned into parasols, and yews fantastically clipped; this luxury of art so skilfully combined with that of nature in Court dress; those cascades over marble steps where the water spreads so shyly, a filmy scarf swept aside by the wind and immediately renewed; those bronzed metal figures speechlessly inhabiting the silent grove; that lordly palace, an object in the landscape from every side, raising its light outline at the foot of the Alps, - all the living thoughts which animate the stone, the bronze, and the trees, or express themselves in garden plots, - this lavish prodigality was in perfect keeping with the loves of a duchess and a handsome youth, for they are a poem far removed from the coarse ends of brutal nature.

Any one with a soul for fantasy would have looked to see, on one of those noble flights of steps, standing by a vase with medallions in bas-relief, a negro boy swathed about the loins with scarlet stuff, and holding in one hand a parasol over the Duchess' head, and in the other the train of her long skirt, while she listened to Emilio Memmi. And how far grander the Venetian would have looked in such a dress as the Senators wore whom Titian painted.

But alas! in this fairy palace, not unlike that of the Peschieri at Genoa, the Duchess Cataneo obeyed the edicts of Victorine and the Paris fashions. She had on a muslin dress and broad straw hat, pretty shot silk shoes, thread lace stockings that a breath of air would have blown away; and over her shoulders a black lace shawl. But the thing which no one could ever understand in Paris, where women are sheathed in their dresses as a dragon-fly is cased in its annular armor, was the perfect freedom with which this lovely daughter of Tuscany wore her French attire; she had Italianized it. A Frenchwoman treats her shirt with the greatest seriousness; an Italian never thinks about it; she does not attempt self-protection by some prim glance, for she knows that she is safe in that of a devoted love, a passion as sacred and serious in her eyes as in those of others.

At eleven in the forenoon, after a walk, and by the side of a table still strewn with the remains of an elegant breakfast, the Duchess, lounging in an easy-chair, left her lover the master of these muslin draperies, without a frown each time he moved. Emilio, seated at her side, held one of her hands between his, gazing at her with utter absorption. Ask not whether they loved; they loved only too well. They were not reading out of the same book, like Paolo and Francesca; far from it, Emilio dared not say: "Let us read." The gleam of those eyes, those glistening gray irises streaked with threads of gold that started from the centre like rifts of light, giving her gaze a soft, star-like radiance, thrilled him with nervous rapture that was almost a spasm. Sometimes the mere sight of the splendid black hair that crowned the adored head, bound by a simple gold fillet, and falling in satin tresses on each side of a spacious brow, was enough to give him a ringing in his ears, the wild tide of the blood rushing through his veins as if it must burst his heart. By what obscure phenomenon did his soul so overmaster his body that he was no longer conscious of his independent self, but was wholly one with this woman at the least word she spoke in that voice which disturbed the very sources of life in him? If, in utter seclusion, a woman of moderate charms can, by being constantly studied, seem supreme and imposing, perhaps one so magnificently handsome as the Duchess could fascinate to stupidity a youth in whom rapture found some fresh incitement; for she had really absorbed his young soul.

Massimilla, the heiress of the Doni, of Florence, had married the Sicilian Duke Cataneo. Her mother, since dead, had hoped, by promoting this marriage, to leave her rich and happy, according to Florentine custom. She had concluded that her daughter, emerging from a convent to embark in life, would achieve, under the laws of love, that second union of heart with heart which, to an Italian woman, is all in all. But Massimilla Doni had acquired in her convent a real taste for a religious life, and, when she had pledged her troth to Duke Cataneo, she was Christianly content to be his wife.

This was an untenable position. Cataneo, who only looked for a duchess, thought himself ridiculous as a husband; and, when Massimilla complained of this indifference, he calmly bid her look about her for a *cavaliere servente*, even offering his services to introduce to her some youths from whom to choose. The Duchess wept; the Duke made his bow.

Massimilla looked about her at the world that crowded round her; her mother took her to the Pergola, to some ambassadors' drawing-rooms, to the Cascine - wherever handsome young men of fashion were to be met; she saw none to her mind, and determined to travel. Then she lost her mother, inherited her property, assumed mourning, and made her way to Venice. There she saw Emilio, who, as he went past her opera box, exchanged with her a flash of inquiry.

This was all. The Venetian was thunderstruck, while a voice in the Duchess' ear called out: "This is he!"

Anywhere else two persons more prudent and less guileless would have studied and examined each other; but these two ignorances mingled like two masses of homogeneous matter, which, when they meet, form but one. Massimilla was at once and thenceforth Venetian. She bought the palazzo she had rented on the Canareggio; and then, not knowing how to invest her wealth, she had purchased Rivalta, the country-place where she was now staying.

Emilio, being introduced to the Duchess by the Signora Vulpato, waited very respectfully on the lady in her box all through the winter. Never was love more ardent in two souls, or more bashful in its advances. The two children were afraid of each other. Massimilla was no coquette. She had no second string to her bow, no *secondo*, no *terzo*, no *patito*. Satisfied with a smile and a word, she admired her Venetian youth, with his pointed face, his long, thin nose, his black eyes, and noble brow; but, in spite of her artless encouragement, he never went to her house till they had spent three months in getting used to each other.

Then summer brought its Eastern sky. The Duchess lamented having to go alone to Rivalta. Emilio, at once happy and uneasy at the thought of being alone with her, had accompanied Massimilla to her retreat. And now this pretty pair had been there for six months.

Massimilla, now twenty, had not sacrificed her religious principles to her passion without a struggle. Still they had yielded, though tardily; and at this moment she would have been ready to consummate the love union for which her mother had prepared her, as Emilio sat there holding her beautiful, aristocratic hand, - long, white, and sheeny, ending in fine, rosy nails, as if she had procured from Asia some of the henna with which the Sultan's wives dye their fingertips.

A misfortune, of which she was unconscious, but which was torture to Emilio, kept up a singular barrier between them. Massimilla, young as she was, had the majestic bearing which mythological tradition ascribes to Juno, the only goddess to whom it does not give a lover; for Diana, the chaste Diana, loved! Jupiter alone could hold his own with his divine better-half, on whom many English ladies model themselves.

Emilio set his mistress far too high ever to touch her. A year hence, perhaps, he might not be a victim to this noble error which attacks none but very young or very old men. But as the archer who shoots beyond the mark is as far from it as he whose arrow falls short of it, the Duchess found herself between a husband who knew he was so far from reaching the target, that he had ceased to try for it, and a lover who was carried so much past it on the white wings of an angel, that he could not get back to it. Massimilla could be happy with desire, not imagining its issue; but her lover, distressful in his happiness, would sometimes obtain from his beloved a promise that led her to the edge of what many women call "the gulf," and thus found himself obliged to be satisfied with plucking the flowers at the edge, incapable of daring more than to pull off their petals, and smother his torture in his heart.

They had wandered out together that morning,

repeating such a hymn of love as the birds warbled in the branches. On their return, the youth, whose situation can only be described by comparing him to the cherubs represented by painters as having only a head and wings, had been so impassioned as to venture to hint a doubt as to the Duchess' entire devotion, so as to bring her to the point of saying: "What proof do you need?"

The question had been asked with a royal air, and Memmi had ardently kissed the beautiful and guileless hand. Then he suddenly started up in a rage with himself, and left the Duchess. Massimilla remained in her indolent attitude on the sofa; but she wept, wondering how, young and handsome as she was, she could fail to please Emilio. Memmi, on the other hand, knocked his head against the tree-trunks like a hooded crow.

But at this moment a servant came in pursuit of the young Venetian to deliver a letter brought by express messenger.

Marco Vendramini, - a name also pronounced Vendramin, in the Venetian dialect, which drops many final letters, - his only friend, wrote to tell him that Facino Cane, Prince of Varese, had died in a hospital in Paris. Proofs of his death had come to hand, and the Cane-Memmi were Princes of Varese. In the eyes of the two young men a title without wealth being worthless, Vendramin also informed Emilio, as a far more important fact, of the engagement at the *Fenice* of the famous tenor Genovese, and the no less famous Signora Tinti.

Without waiting to finish the letter, which he crumpled

up and put in his pocket, Emilio ran to communicate this great news to the Duchess, forgetting his heraldic honors.

The Duchess knew nothing of the strange story which made la Tinti an object of curiosity in Italy, and Emilio briefly repeated it.

This illustrious singer had been a mere inn-servant, whose wonderful voice had captivated a great Sicilian nobleman on his travels. The girl's beauty - she was then twelve years old - being worthy of her voice, the gentleman had had the moderation to have brought her up, as Louis XV. had Mademoiselle de Romans educated. He had waited patiently till Clara's voice had been fully trained by a famous professor, and till she was sixteen, before taking toll of the treasure so carefully cultivated.

La Tinti had made her debut the year before, and had enchanted the three most fastidious capitals of Italy.

"I am perfectly certain that her great nobleman is not my husband," said the Duchess.

The horses were ordered, and the Duchess set out at once for Venice, to be present at the opening of the winter season.

So one fine evening in November, the new Prince of Varese was crossing the lagoon from Mestre to Venice, between the lines of stakes painted with Austrian colors, which mark out the channel for gondolas as conceded by the custom-house. As he watched Massimilla's gondola, navigated by men in livery, and cutting through the water a few yards in front, poor

Emilio, with only an old gondolier who had been his father's servant in the days when Venice was still a living city, could not repress the bitter reflections suggested to him by the assumption of his title.

"What a mockery of fortune! A prince - with fifteen hundred francs a year! Master of one of the finest palaces in the world, and unable to sell the statues, stairs, paintings, sculpture, which an Austrian decree had made inalienable! To live on a foundation of piles of campeachy wood worth nearly a million of francs, and have no furniture! To own sumptuous galleries, and live in an attic above the topmost arabesque cornice constructed of marble brought from the Morea - the land which a Memmius had marched over as conqueror in the time of the Romans! To see his ancestors in effigy on their tombs of precious marbles in one of the most splendid churches in Venice, and in a chapel graced with pictures by Titian and Tintoretto, by Palma, Bellini, Paul Veronese - and to be prohibited from selling a marble Memmi to the English for bread for the living Prince Varese! Genovese, the famous tenor, could get in one season, by his warbling, the capital of an income on which this son of the Memmi could live - this descendant of Roman senators as venerable as Caesar and Sylla. Genovese may smoke an Eastern hookah, and the Prince of Varese cannot even have enough cigars!"

He tossed the end he was smoking into the sea. The Prince of Varese found cigars at the Duchess Cataneo's; how gladly would he have laid the treasures of the world at her feet! She studied all his caprices, and was happy to gratify them. He made his only meal at her house - his supper; for all his money was spent in clothes and his place in the *Fenice*. He had also to pay a hundred francs a year as wages to his father's old gondolier; and he, to serve him for that sum, had to live exclusively on rice. Also he kept enough to take a cup of black coffee every morning at Florian's to keep himself up till the evening in a state of nervous excitement, and this habit, carried to excess, he hoped would in due time kill him, as Vendramin relied on opium.

"And I am a prince!"

As he spoke the words, Emilio Memmi tossed Marco Vendramin's letter into the lagoon without even reading it to the end, and it floated away like a paper boat launched by a child.

"But Emilio," he went on to himself, "is but three and twenty. He is a better man than Lord Wellington with the gout, than the paralyzed Regent, than the epileptic royal family of Austria, than the King of France -"

But as he thought of the King of France Emilio's brow was knit, his ivory skin burned yellower, tears gathered in his black eyes and hung to his long lashes; he raised a hand worthy to be painted by Titian to push back his thick brown hair, and gazed again at Massimilla's gondola.

"And this insolent mockery of fate is carried even into my love affair," said he to himself. "My heart and imagination are full of precious gifts; Massimilla will have none of them; she is a Florentine, and she will throw me over. I have to sit by her side like ice, while her voice and her looks fire me with heavenly sensations! As I watch her gondola a few hundred feet away from my own I feel as if a hot iron were set on my heart. An invisible fluid courses through my frame and scorches my nerves, a cloud dims my sight, the air seems to me to glow as it did at Rivalta when the sunlight came through a red silk blind, and I, without her knowing it, could admire her lost in dreams, with her subtle smile like that of Leonardo's Mona Lisa. Well, either my Highness will end my days by a pistol-shot, or the heir of the Cane will follow old Carmagnola's advice; we will be sailors, pirates; and it will be amusing to see how long we can live without being hanged."

The Prince lighted another cigar, and watched the curls of smoke as the wind wafted them away, as though he saw in their arabesques an echo of this last thought.

In the distance he could now perceive the mauresque pinnacles that crowned his palazzo, and he was sadder than ever. The Duchess' gondola had vanished in the Canareggio.

These fantastic pictures of a romantic and perilous existence, as the outcome of his love, went out with his cigar, and his lady's gondola no longer traced his path. Then he saw the present in its real light: a palace without a soul, a soul that had no effect on the body, a principality without money, an empty body and a full heart - a thousand heartbreaking contradictions. The hapless youth mourned for Venice as she had been, - as did Vendramini, even more bitterly, for it was a great and common sorrow, a similar destiny, that had engendered such a warm friendship between these two young men, the wreckage of two illustrious families.

Emilio could not help dreaming of a time when the palazzo Memmi poured out light from every window, and rang with music carried far away over the Adriatic tide; when hundreds of gondolas might be seen tied up to its mooring-posts, while graceful masked figures and the magnates of the Republic crowded up the steps kissed by the waters; when its halls and gallery were full of a throng of intriguers or their dupes; when the great banqueting-hall, filled with merry feasters, and the upper balconies furnished with musicians, seemed to harbor all Venice coming and going on the great staircase that rang with laughter.

The chisels of the greatest artists of many centuries had sculptured the bronze brackets supporting long-necked or pot-bellied Chinese vases, and the candelabra for a thousand tapers. Every country had furnished some contribution to the splendor that decked the walls and ceilings. But now the panels were stripped of the handsome hangings, the melancholy ceilings were speechless and sad. No Turkey carpets, no lustres bright with flowers, no statues, no pictures, no more joy, no money - the great means to enjoyment! Venice, the London of the Middle Ages, was falling stone by stone, man by man. The ominous green weed which the sea washes and kisses at the foot of every palace, was in the Prince's eyes, a black fringe hung by nature as an omen of death.

And finally, a great English poet had rushed down on Venice like a raven on a corpse, to croak out in lyric poetry - the first and last utterance of social man - the burden of a *de profundis*. English poetry! Flung in the face of the city that had given birth to Italian poetry! Poor Venice!

Conceive, then, of the young man's amazement when roused from such meditations by Carmagnola's cry:

Honore de Balzac

"Serenissimo, the palazzo is on fire, or the old Doges have risen from their tombs! There are lights in the windows of the upper floor!"

Prince Emilio fancied that his dream was realized by the touch of a magic wand. It was dusk, and the old gondolier could by tying up his gondola to the top step, help his young master to land without being seen by the bustling servants in the palazzo, some of whom were buzzing about the landing-place like bees at the door of a hive. Emilio stole into the great hall, whence rose the finest flight of stairs in all Venice, up which he lightly ran to investigate the cause of this strange bustle.

A whole tribe of workmen were hurriedly completing the furnishing and redecoration of the palace. The first floor, worthy of the antique glories of Venice, displayed to Emilio's waking eyes the magnificence of which he had just been dreaming, and the fairy had exercised admirable taste. Splendor worthy of a parvenu sovereign was to be seen even in the smallest details. Emilio wandered about without remark from anybody, and surprise followed on surprise.

Curious, then, to know what was going forward on the second floor, he went up, and found everything finished. The unknown laborers, commissioned by a wizard to revive the marvels of the Arabian nights in behalf of an impoverished Italian prince, were exchanging some inferior articles of furniture brought in for the nonce. Prince Emilio made his way into the bedroom, which smiled on him like a shell just deserted by Venus. The room was so charmingly pretty, so daintily smart, so full of elegant contrivance, that he straightway seated himself in an armchair of gilt wood, in front of which a most appetizing cold supper stood ready, and, without more ado, proceeded to eat.

"In all the world there is no one but Massimilla who would have thought of this surprise," thought he. "She heard that I was now a prince; Duke Cataneo is perhaps dead, and has left her his fortune; she is twice as rich as she was; she will marry me -"

And he ate in a way that would have roused the envy of an invalid Croesus, if he could have seen him; and he drank floods of capital port wine.

"Now I understand the knowing little air she put on as she said, 'Till this evening!' Perhaps she means to come and break the spell. What a fine bed! and in the bed-place such a pretty lamp! Quite a Florentine idea!"

There are some strongly blended natures on which extremes of joy or of grief have a soporific effect. Now on a youth so compounded that he could idealize his mistress to the point of ceasing to think of her as a woman, this sudden incursion of wealth had the effect of a dose of opium. When the Prince had drunk the whole of the bottle of port, eaten half a fish and some portion of a French pate, he felt an irresistible longing for bed. Perhaps he was suffering from a double intoxication. So he pulled off the counterpane, opened the bed, undressed in a pretty dressing-room, and lay down to meditate on destiny.

"I forgot poor Carmagnola," said he; "but my cook and butler will have provided for him."

At this juncture, a waiting-woman came in, lightly

Honore de Balzac

humming an air from the *Barbiere*. She tossed a woman's dress on a chair, a whole outfit for the night, and said as she did so:

"Here they come!"

And in fact a few minutes later a young lady came in, dressed in the latest French style, who might have sat for some English fancy portrait engraved for a *Forget-me-not*, a *Belle Assemblee*, or a *Book of Beauty*.

The Prince shivered with delight and with fear, for, as you know, he was in love with Massimilla. But, in spite of this faith in love which fired his blood, and which of old inspired the painters of Spain, which gave Italy her Madonnas, created Michael Angelo's statues and Ghilberti's doors of the Baptistery, - desire had him in its toils, and agitated him without infusing into his heart that warm, ethereal glow which he felt at a look or a word from the Duchess. His soul, his heart, his reason, every impulse of his will, revolted at the thought of an infidelity; and yet that brutal, unreasoning infidelity domineered over his spirit. But the woman was not alone.

The Prince saw one of those figures in which nobody believes when they are transferred from real life, where we wonder at them, to the imaginary existence of a more or less literary description. The dress of this stranger, like that of all Neapolitans, displayed five colors, if the black of his hat may count for a color; his trousers were olive-brown, his red waistcoat shone with gilt buttons, his coat was greenish, and his linen was more yellow than white. This personage seemed to have made it his business to verify the Neapolitan as represented by Gerolamo on the stage of his puppet show. His eyes looked like glass beads. His nose, like the ace of clubs, was horribly long and bulbous; in fact, it did its best to conceal an opening which it would be an insult to the human countenance to call a mouth; within, three or four tusks were visible, endowed, as it seemed, with a proper motion and fitting into each other. His fleshy ears drooped by their own weight, giving the creature a whimsical resemblance to a dog.

His complexion, tainted, no doubt, by various metallic infusions as prescribed by some Hippocrates, verged on black. A pointed skull, scarcely covered by a few straight hairs like spun glass, crowned this forbidding face with red spots. Finally, though the man was very thin and of medium height, he had long arms and broad shoulders.

In spite of these hideous details, and though he looked fully seventy, he did not lack a certain cyclopean dignity; he had aristocratic manners and the confident demeanor of a rich man.

Any one who could have found courage enough to study him, would have seen his history written by base passions on this noble clay degraded to mud. Here was the man of high birth, who, rich from his earliest youth, had given up his body to debauchery for the sake of extravagant enjoyment. And debauchery had destroyed the human being and made another after its own image. Thousands of bottles of wine had disappeared under the purple archway of that preposterous nose, and left their dregs on his lips. Long and slow digestion had destroyed his teeth. His eyes had grown dim under the lamps of the gaming table. The blood tainted with impurities had vitiated the nervous system.

The expenditure of force in the task of digestion had undermined his intellect. Finally, amours had thinned his hair. Each vice, like a greedy heir, had stamped possession on some part of the living body.

Those who watch nature detect her in jests of the shrewdest irony. For instance, she places toads in the neighborhood of flowers, as she had placed this man by the side of this rose of love.

"Will you play the violin this evening, my dear Duke?" asked the woman, as she unhooked a cord to let a handsome curtain fall over the door.

"Play the violin!" thought Prince Emilio. "What can have happened to my palazzo? Am I awake? Here I am, in that woman's bed, and she certainly thinks herself at home - she has taken off her cloak! Have I, like Vendramin, inhaled opium, and am I in the midst of one of those dreams in which he sees Venice as it was three centuries ago?"

The unknown fair one, seated in front of a dressing-table blazing with wax lights, was unfastening her frippery with the utmost calmness.

"Ring for Giulia," said she; "I want to get my dress off."

At that instant, the Duke noticed that the supper had been disturbed; he looked round the room, and discovered the Prince's trousers hanging over a chair at the foot of the bed.

"Clarina, I will not ring!" cried the Duke, in a shrill voice of fury. "I will not play the violin this evening, nor tomorrow, nor ever again -"

"Ta, ta, ta, ta!" sang Clarina, on the four octaves of the same note, leaping from one to the next with the ease of a nightingale.

"In spite of that voice, which would make your patron saint Clara envious, you are really too impudent, you rascally hussy!"

"You have not brought me up to listen to such abuse," said she, with some pride.

"Have I brought you up to hide a man in your bed? You are unworthy alike of my generosity and of my hatred -"

"A man in my bed!" exclaimed Clarina, hastily looking round.

"And after daring to eat our supper, as if he were at home," added the Duke.

"But am I not at home?" cried Emilio. "I am the Prince of Varese; this palace is mine."

As he spoke, Emilio sat up in bed, his handsome and noble Venetian head framed in the flowing hangings.

At first Clarina laughed - one of those irrepressible fits of laughter which seize a girl when she meets with an adventure comic beyond all conception. But her laughter ceased as she saw the young man, who, as has been said, was remarkably handsome, though but lightly attired; the madness that possessed Emilio seized her, too, and, as she had no one to adore, no sense of reason bridled her sudden fancy - a Sicilian woman in love.

"Although this is the palazzo Memmi, I will thank your Highness to quit," said the Duke, assuming the cold irony of a polished gentleman. "I am at home here."

"Let me tell you, Monsieur le Duc, that you are in my room, not in your own," said Clarina, rousing herself from her amazement. "If you have any doubts of my virtue, at any rate give me the benefit of my crime -"

"Doubts! Say proof positive, my lady!"

"I swear to you that I am innocent," replied Clarina.

"What, then, do I see in that bed?" asked the Duke.

"Old Ogre!" cried Clarina. "If you believe your eyes rather than my assertion, you have ceased to love me. Go, and do not weary my ears! Do you hear? Go, Monsieur le Duc. This young Prince will repay you the million francs I have cost you, if you insist."

"I will repay nothing," said Emilio in an undertone.

"There is nothing due! A million is cheap for Clara Tinti when a man is so ugly. Now, go," said she to the Duke. "You dismissed me; now I dismiss you. We are quits."

At a gesture on Cataneo's part, as he seemed inclined to dispute this order, which was given with an action worthy of Semiramis, - the part in which la Tinti had won her fame, - the prima donna flew at the old ape and put him out of the room.

"If you do not leave me in quiet this evening, we never meet again. And my *never* counts for more than yours," she added.

"Quiet!" retorted the Duke, with a bitter laugh. "Dear idol, it strikes me that I am leaving you *agitata*!"

The Duke departed.

His mean spirit was no surprise to Emilio.

Every man who has accustomed himself to some particular taste, chosen from among the various effects of love, in harmony with his own nature, knows that no consideration can stop a man who has allowed his passions to become a habit.

Clarina bounded like a fawn from the door to the bed.

"A prince, and poor, young, and handsome!" cried she. "Why, it is a fairy tale!"

The Sicilian perched herself on the bed with the artless freedom of an animal, the yearning of a plant for the sun, the airy motion of a branch waltzing to the breeze. As she unbuttoned the wristbands of her sleeves, she began to sing, not in the pitch that won her the applause of an audience at the *Fenice*, but in a warble tender with emotion. Her song was a zephyr carrying the caresses of her love to the heart.

She stole a glance at Emilio, who was as much embarrassed as she; for this woman of the stage had lost all the boldness that had sparkled in her eyes and given decision to her voice and gestures when she dismissed the Duke. She was as humble as a courtesan who has fallen in love.

To picture la Tinti you must recall one of our best French singers when she came out in *Il Fazzoletto*, an opera by Garcia that was then being played by an Italian company at the theatre in the Rue Lauvois. She was so beautiful that a Naples guardsman, having failed to win a hearing, killed himself in despair. The prima donna of the *Fenice* had the same refinement of features, the same elegant figure, and was equally young; but she had in addition the warm blood of Sicily that gave a glow to her loveliness. Her voice was fuller and richer, and she had that air of native majesty that is characteristic of Italian women.

La Tinti - whose name also resembled that which the French singer assumed - was now seventeen, and the poor Prince three-and-twenty. What mocking hand had thought it sport to bring the match so near the powder? A fragrant room hung with rose-colored silk and brilliant with wax lights, a bed dressed in lace, a silent palace, and Venice! Two young and beautiful creatures! every ravishment at once.

Emilio snatched up his trousers, jumped out of bed, escaped into the dressing-room, put on his clothes, came back and hurried to the door.

These were his thoughts while dressing: -

"Massimilla, beloved daughter of the Doni, in whom Italian beauty is an hereditary prerogative, you who are worthy of the portrait of *Margherita*, one of the few canvases painted entirely by Raphael to his glory! My beautiful and saintly mistress, shall I not have deserved you if I fly from this abyss of flowers? Should I be worthy of you if I profaned a heart that is wholly yours? No; I will not fall into the vulgar snare laid for me by my rebellious senses! This girl has her Duke, mine be my Duchess!"

As he lifted the curtain, he heard a moan. The heroic lover looked round and saw Clarina on her knees, her face hidden in the bed, choking with sobs. Is it to be believed? The singer was lovelier kneeling thus, her face invisible, than even in her confusion with a glowing countenance. Her hair, which had fallen over her shoulders, her Magdalen-like attitude, the disorder of her half-unfastened dress, - the whole picture had been composed by the devil, who, as is well known, is a fine colorist.

The Prince put his arm round the weeping girl, who slipped from him like a snake, and clung to one foot, pressing it to her beautiful bosom.

"Will you explain to me," said he, shaking his foot to free it from her embrace, "how you happen to be in my palazzo? How the impoverished Emilio Memmi -"

"Emilio Memmi!" cried Tinti, rising. "You said you were a Prince."

"A Prince since yesterday."

"You are in love with the Duchess Cataneo!" said she, looking at him from head to foot.

Emilio stood mute, seeing that the prima dona was smiling at him through her tears.

"Your Highness does not know that the man who had

me trained for the stage - that the Duke - is Cataneo himself. And your friend Vendramini, thinking to do you a service, let him this palace for a thousand crowns, for the period of my season at the *Fenice*. Dear idol of my heart!" she went on, taking his hand and drawing him towards her, "why do you fly from one for whom many a man would run the risk of broken bones? Love, you see, is always love. It is the same everywhere; it is the sun of our souls; we can warm ourselves whenever it shines, and here - now - it is full noonday. If to-morrow you are not satisfied, kill me! But I shall survive, for I am a real beauty!"

Emilio decided on remaining. When he signified his consent by a nod the impulse of delight that sent a shiver through Clarina seemed to him like a light from hell. Love had never before appeared to him in so impressive a form.

At that moment Carmagnola whistled loudly.

"What can he want of me?" said the Prince.

But bewildered by love, Emilio paid no heed to the gondolier's repeated signals.

If you have never traveled in Switzerland you may perhaps read this description with pleasure; and if you have clambered among those mountains you will not be sorry to be reminded of the scenery.

In that sublime land, in the heart of a mass of rock riven by a gorge, - a valley as wide as the Avenue de Neuilly in Paris, but a hundred fathoms deep and broken into ravines, - flows a torrent coming from some tremendous height of the Saint-Gothard on the

Simplon, which has formed a pool, I know not how many yards deep or how many feet long and wide, hemmed in by splintered cliffs of granite on which meadows find a place, with fir-trees between them, and enormous elms, and where violets also grow, and strawberries. Here and there stands a chalet and at the window you may see the rosy face of a yellow-haired Swiss girl. According to the moods of the sky the water in this tarn is blue and green, but as a sapphire is blue, as an emerald is green. Well, nothing in the world can give such an idea of depth, peace, immensity, heavenly love, and eternal happiness - to the most heedless traveler, the most hurried courier, the most commonplace tradesman - as this liquid diamond into which the snow, gathering from the highest Alps, trickles through a natural channel hidden under the trees and eaten through the rock, escaping below through a gap without a sound. The watery sheet over-hanging the fall glides so gently that no ripple is to be seen on the surface which mirrors the chaise as you drive past. The postboy smacks his whip; you turn past a crag; you cross a bridge: suddenly there is a terrific uproar of cascades tumbling together one upon another. The water, taking a mighty leap, is broken into a hundred falls, dashed to spray on the boulders; it sparkles in a myriad jets against a mass that has fallen from the heights that tower over the ravine exactly in the middle of the road that has been so irresistibly cut by the most formidable of active forces.

If you have formed a clear idea of this landscape, you will see in those sleeping waters the image of Emilio's love for the Duchess, and in the cascades leaping like a flock of sheep, an idea of his passion shared with la Tinti. In the midst of his torrent of love a rock stood up against which the torrent broke. The Prince, like

Sisyphus, was constantly under the stone.

"What on earth does the Duke do with a violin?" he wondered. "Do I owe this symphony to him?"

He asked Clara Tinti.

"My dear child," - for she saw that Emilio was but a child, - "dear child," said she, "that man, who is a hundred and eighteen in the parish register of vice, and only forty-seven in the register of the Church, has but one single joy left to him in life. Yes, everything is broken, everything in him is ruin or rags; his soul, intellect, heart, nerves, - everything in man that can supply an impulse and remind him of heaven, either by desire or enjoyment, is bound up with music, or rather with one of the many effects produced by music, the perfect unison of two voices, or of a voice with the top string of his violin. The old ape sits on my knee, takes his instrument, - he plays fairly well, - he produces the notes, and I try to imitate them. Then, when the long-sought-for moment comes when it is impossible to distinguish in the body of sound which is the note on the violin and which proceeds from my throat, the old man falls into an ecstasy, his dim eyes light up with their last remaining fires, he is quite happy and will roll on the floor like a drunken man.

"That is why he pays Genovese such a price. Genovese is the only tenor whose voice occasionally sounds in unison with mine. Either we really do sing exactly together once or twice in an evening, or the Duke imagines that we do; and for that imaginary pleasure he has bought Genovese. Genovese belongs to him. No theatrical manager can engage that tenor without me, nor have me to sing without him. The Duke brought me up on purpose to gratify that whim; to him I owe my talent, my beauty, - my fortune, no doubt. He will die of an attack of perfect unison. The sense of hearing alone has survived the wreck of his faculties; that is the only thread by which he holds on to life. A vigorous shoot springs from that rotten stump. There are, I am told, many men in the same predicament. May Madonna preserve them!

"You have not come to that! You can do all you want - all I want of you, I know."

Towards morning the Prince stole away and found Carmagnola lying asleep across the door.

"Altezza," said the gondolier, "the Duchess ordered me to give you this note."

He held out a dainty sheet of paper folded into a triangle. The Prince felt dizzy; he went back into the room and dropped into a chair, for his sight was dim, and his hands shook as he read: -

"DEAR EMILIO: - Your gondola stopped at your palazzo. Did you not know that Cataneo has taken it for la Tinti? If you love me, go to-night to Vendramin, who tells me he has a room ready for you in his house. What shall I do? Can I remain in Venice to see my husband and his opera singer? Shall we go back together to Friuli? Write me one word, if only to tell me what the letter was you tossed into the lagoon.

"MASSIMILLA DONI."

The writing and the scent of the paper brought a

thousand memories back to the young Venetian's mind. The sun of a single-minded passion threw its radiance on the blue depths come from so far, collected in a bottomless pool, and shining like a star. The noble youth could not restrain the tears that flowed freely from his eyes, for in the languid state produced by satiated senses he was disarmed by the thought of that purer divinity.

Even in her sleep Clarina heard his weeping; she sat up in bed, saw her Prince in a dejected attitude, and threw herself at his knees.

"They are still waiting for the answer," said Carmagnola, putting the curtain aside.

"Wretch, you have undone me!" cried Emilio, starting up and spurning Clarina with his foot.

She clutched it so lovingly, her look imploring some explanation, - the look of a tear-stained Samaritan, - that Emilio, enraged to find himself still in the toils of the passion that had wrought his fall, pushed away the singer with an unmanly kick.

"You told me to kill you, - then die, venomous reptile!" he exclaimed.

He left the palace, and sprang into his gondola.

"Pull," said he to Carmagnola.

"Where?" asked the old servant.

"Where you will."

The gondolier divined his master's wishes, and by many windings brought him at last into the Canareggio, to the door of a wonderful palazzo, which you will admire when you see Venice, for no traveler ever fails to stop in front of those windows, each of a different design, vying with each other in fantastic ornament, with balconies like lace-work; to study the corners finishing in tall and slender twisted columns, the string-courses wrought by so inventive a chisel that no two shapes are alike in the arabesques on the stones.

How charming is that doorway! how mysterious the vaulted arcade leading to the stairs! Who could fail to admire the steps on which ingenious art has laid a carpet that will last while Venice stands, - a carpet as rich as if wrought in Turkey, but composed of marbles in endless variety of shapes, inlaid in white marble. You will delight in the charming ornament of the colonnades of the upper story, - gilt like those of a ducal palace, - so that the marvels of art are both under your feet and above your head.

What delicate shadows! How silent, how cool! But how solemn, too, was that old palace! where, to delight Emilio and his friend Vendramin, the Duchess had collected antique Venetian furniture, and employed skilled hands to restore the ceilings. There, old Venice lived again. The splendor was not merely noble, it was instructive. The archaeologist would have found there such models of perfection as the middle ages produced, having taken example from Venice. Here were to be seen the original ceilings of woodwork covered with scrolls and flowers in gold on a colored ground, or in colors on gold, and ceilings of gilt plaster castings, with a picture of many figures in each corner, with a splendid fresco in the centre, - a style so costly that

Honore de Balzac

there are not two in the Louvre, and that the extravagance of Louis XIV. shrunk from such expense at Versailles. On all sides marble, wood, and silk had served as materials for exquisite workmanship.

Emilio pushed open a carved oak door, made his way down the long, vaulted passage which runs from end to end on each floor of a Venetian palazzo, and stopped before another door, so familiar that it made his heart beat. On seeing him, a lady companion came out of a vast drawing-room, and admitted him to a study where he found the Duchess on her knees in front of a Madonna.

He had come to confess and ask forgiveness. Massimilla, in prayer, had converted him. He and God; nothing else dwelt in that heart.

The Duchess rose very unaffectedly, and held out her hand. Her lover did not take it.

"Did not Gianbattista see you, yesterday?" she asked.

"No," he replied.

"That piece of ill-luck gave me a night of misery. I was so afraid lest you might meet the Duke, whose perversity I know too well. What made Vendramin let your palace to him?"

"It was a good idea, Milla, for your Prince is poor enough."

Massimilla was so beautiful in her trust of him, and so wonderfully lovely, so happy in Emilio's presence, that at this moment the Prince, wide awake, experienced the sensations of the horrible dream that torments persons of a lively imagination, in which after arriving in a ballroom full of women in full dress, the dreamer is suddenly aware that he is naked, without even a shirt; shame and terror possess him by turns, and only waking can relieve him from his misery. Thus stood Emilio's soul in the presence of his mistress. Hitherto that soul had known only the fairest flowers of feeling; a debauch had plunged it into dishonor. This none knew but he, for the beautiful Florentine ascribed so many virtues to her lover that the man she adored could not but be incapable of any stain.

As Emilio had not taken her hand, the Duchess pushed her fingers through his hair that the singer had kissed. Then she perceived that Emilio's hand was clammy and his brow moist.

"What ails you?" she asked, in a voice to which tenderness gave the sweetness of a flute.

"Never till this moment have I known how much I love you," he replied.

"Well, dear idol, what would you have?" said she.

"What have I done to make her ask that?" he wondered to himself.

"Emilio, what letter was that which you threw into the lagoon?"

"Vendramini's. I had not read it to the end, or I should never have gone to my palazzo, and there have met the Duke; for no doubt it told me all about it."

Massimilla turned pale, but a caress from Emilio reassured her.

"Stay with me all day; we will go to the opera together. We will not set out for Friuli; your presence will no doubt enable me to endure Cataneo's," said Massimilla.

Though this would be torment to her lover's soul, he consented with apparent joy.

If anything can give us a foretaste of what the damned will suffer on finding themselves so unworthy of God, is it not the state of a young man, as yet unpolluted, in the presence of a mistress he reveres, while he still feels on his lips the taste of infidelity, and brings into the sanctuary of the divinity he worships the tainted atmosphere of the courtesan?

Baader, who in his lectures eliminated things divine by erotic imagery, had no doubt observed, like some Catholic writers, the intimate resemblance between human and heavenly love.

This distress of mind cast a hue of melancholy over the pleasure the young Venetian felt in his mistress' presence. A woman's instinct has amazing aptitude for harmony of feeling; it assumes the hue, it vibrates to the note suggested by her lover. The pungent flavor of coquettish spice is far indeed from spurring affection so much as this gentle sympathy of tenderness. The smartness of a coquette too clearly marks opposition; however transient it is displeasing; but this intimate comprehension shows a perfect fusion of souls. The hapless Emilio was touched by the unspoken divination which led the Duchess to pity a fault unknown to her.

Massimilla, feeling that her strength lay in the absence of any sensual side to her love, could allow herself to be expansive; she boldly and confidently poured out her angelic spirit, she stripped it bare, just as during that diabolical night, La Tinti had displayed the soft lines of her body, and her firm, elastic flesh. In Emilio's eyes there was as it were a conflict between the saintly love of this white soul and that of the vehement and muscular Sicilian.

The day was spent in long looks following on deep meditations. Each of them gauged the depths of tender feeling, and found it bottomless; a conviction that brought fond words to their lips. Modesty, the goddess who in a moment of forgetfulness with Love, was the mother of Coquettishness, need not have put her hand before her face as she looked at these lovers. As a crowning joy, an orgy of happiness, Massimilla pillowed Emilio's head in her arms, and now and then ventured to press her lips to his; but only as a bird dips its beak into the clear waters of a spring, looking round lest it should be seen. Their fancy worked upon this kiss, as a composer develops a subject by the endless resources of music, and it produced in them such tumultuous and vibrating echoes as fevered their blood.

The Idea must always be stronger than the Fact, otherwise desire would be less perfect than satisfaction, and it is in fact the stronger, - it gives birth to wit. And, indeed, they were perfectly happy; for enjoyment must always take something off happiness. Married in heaven alone, these two lovers admired each other in their purest aspect, - that of two souls incandescent, and united in celestial light, radiant to the eyes that faith has touched; and, above all, filled with the rapture which the brush of a Raphael, a Titian, a Murillo, has depicted, and which those who have ever known it, taste again as they gaze at those paintings. Do not such peerless spirits scorn the coarser joys lavished by the Sicilian singer - the material expression of that angelic union?

These noble thoughts were in the Prince's mind as he reposed in heavenly calm on Massimilla's cool, soft, white bosom, under the gentle radiance of her eyes veiled by long, bright lashes; and he gave himself up to this dream of an ideal orgy. At such a moment, Massimilla was as one of the Virgin visions seen in dreams, which vanish at cock-crow, but whom we recognize when we find them again in their realm of glory, - in the works of some great painters of Heaven.

In the evening the lovers went to the theatre. This is the way of Italian life: love in the morning; music in the evening; the night for sleep. How far preferable is this existence to that of a country where every one expends his lungs and strength in politics, without contributing any more, single-minded, to the progress of affairs than a grain of sand can make a cloud of dust. Liberty, in those strange lands, consists in the right to squabble over public concerns, to take care of oneself, to waste time in patriotic undertakings each more futile than the last, inasmuch as they all weaken that noble, holy self-concern which is the parent of all great human achievement. At Venice, on the contrary, love and its myriad ties, the sweet business of real happiness, fills up all the time.

In that country, love is so much a matter of course that the Duchess was regarded as a wonder; for, in spite of her violent attachment to Emilio, everybody was confident of her immaculate purity. And women gave their sincere pity to the poor young man, who was regarded as a victim to the virtue of his lady-love. At the same time, no one cared to blame the Duchess, for in Italy religion is a power as much respected as love.

Evening after evening Massimilla's box was the first object of every opera-glass, and each woman would say to her lover, as she studied the Duchess and her adorer:

"How far have they got?"

The lover would examine Emilio, seeking some evidence of success; would find no expression but that of a pure and dejected passion. And throughout the house, as they visited from box to box, the men would say to the ladies:

"La Cataneo is not yet Emilio's."

"She is unwise," said the old women. "She will tire him out."

"*Forse!*" (Perhaps) the young wives would reply, with the solemn accent that Italians can infuse into that great word - the answer to many questions here below.

Some women were indignant, thought the whole thing ill-judged, and declared that it was a misapprehension of religion to allow it to smother love.

"My dear, love that poor Emilio," said the Signora Vulpato to Massimilla, as they met on the stairs in going out.

"I do love him with all my might," replied the Duchess.

"Then why does not he look happy?"

Massimilla's reply was a little shrug of her shoulders.

We in France - France as the growing mania for English proprieties has made it - can form no idea of the serious interest taken in this affair by Venetian society.

Vendramini alone knew Emilio's secret, which was carefully kept between two men who had, for private pleasure, combined their coats of arms with the motto *Non amici, frates.*

The opening night of the opera season is an event at Venice, as in every capital in Italy. The *Fenice* was crowded.

The five hours of the night that are spent at the theatre fill so important a place in Italian life that it is well to give an account of the customs that have risen from this manner of spending time.

The boxes in Italy are unlike those of any other country, inasmuch as that elsewhere the women go to be seen, and that Italian ladies do not care to make a show of themselves. Each box is long and narrow, sloping at an angle to the front and to the passage behind. On each side is a sofa, and at the end stand two armchairs, one for the mistress of the box, and the other for a lady friend when she brings one, which she rarely does. Each lady is in fact too much engaged in her own box to call on others, or to wish to see them;

also no one cares to introduce a rival. An Italian woman almost always reigns alone in her box; the mothers are not the slaves of their daughters, the daughters have no mother on their hands; thus there are no children, no relations to watch and censure and bore, or cut into a conversation.

In front every box is draped in the same way, with the same silk: from the cornice hang curtains, also all to match; and these remain drawn when the family to whom the box belongs is in mourning. With very few exceptions, and those only at Milan, there is no light inside the box; they are illuminated only from the stage, and from a not very brilliant hanging lustre which, in spite of protests, has been introduced into the house in some towns; still, screened by the curtains, they are never very light, and their arrangement leaves the back of the box so dark that it is very difficult to see what is going on.

The boxes, large enough to accommodate eight or ten persons, are decorated with handsome silks, the ceilings are painted and ornamented in light and pleasing colors; the woodwork is gilt. Ices and sorbets are served there, and sweetmeats; for only the plebeian classes ever have a serious meal. Each box is freehold property, and of considerable value; some are estimated at as much as thirty thousand lire; the Litta family at Milan own three adjoining. These facts sufficiently indicate the importance attributed to this incident of fashionable life.

Conversation reigns supreme in this little apartment, which Stendhal, one of the most ingenious of modern writers, and a keen student of Italian manners, has called a boudoir with a window opening on to a pit.

The music and the spectacle are in fact purely accessory; the real interest of the evening is in the social meeting there, the all-important trivialities of love that are discussed, the assignations held, the anecdotes and gossip that creep in. The theatre is an inexpensive meeting-place for a whole society which is content and amused with studying itself.

The men who are admitted take their seats on one of the sofas, in the order of their arrival. The first comer naturally is next to the mistress of the box, but when both seats are full, if another visitor comes in, the one who has sat longest rises, takes his leave and departs. All move up one place, and so each in turn is next the sovereign.

This futile gossip, or serious colloquy, these elegant trivialities of Italian life, inevitably imply some general intimacy. The lady may be in full dress or not, as she pleases. She is so completely at home that a stranger who has been received in her box may call on her next day at her residence. The foreign visitor cannot at first understand this life of idle wit, this *dolce far niente* on a background of music. Only long custom and keen observation can ever reveal to a foreigner the meaning of Italian life, which is like the free sky of the south, and where a rich man will not endure a cloud. A man of rank cares little about the management of his fortune; he leaves the details to his stewards (ragionati), who rob and ruin him. He has no instinct for politics, and they would presently bore him; he lives exclusively for passion, which fills up all his time; hence the necessity felt by the lady and her lover for being constantly together; for the great feature of such a life is the lover, who for five hours is kept under the eye of a woman who has had him at her feet all day. Thus Italian habits allow of perpetual satisfaction, and necessitate a constant study of the means fitted to insure it, though hidden under apparent light-heartedness.

It is a beautiful life, but a reckless one, and in no country in the world are men so often found worn out.

The Duchess' box was on the pit tier - *pepiano*, as it is called in Venice; she always sat where the light from the stage fell on her face, so that her handsome head, softly illuminated, stood out against the dark background. The Florentine attracted every gaze by her broad, high brow, as white as snow, crowned with plaits of black hair that gave her a really royal look; by the refinement of her features, resembling the noble features of Andrea del Sarto's heads; by the outline of her face, the setting of her eyes; and by those velvet eyes themselves, which spoke of the rapture of a woman dreaming of happiness, still pure though loving, at once attractive and dignified.

Instead of *Mose*, in which la Tinti was to have appeared with Genovese, *Il Barbiere* was given, and the tenor was to sing without the celebrated prima donna. The manager announced that he had been obliged to change the opera in consequence of la Tinti's being ill; and the Duke was not to be seen in the theatre.

Was this a clever trick on the part of the management, to secure two full houses by bringing out Genovese and Tinti separately, or was Clarina's indisposition genuine? While this was open to discussion by others, Emilio might be better informed; and though the announcement caused him some remorse, as he remembered the singer's beauty and vehemence, her absence and the Duke's put both the Prince and the Duchess very much at their ease.

And Genovese sang in such a way as to drive out all memories of a night of illicit love, and to prolong the heavenly joys of this blissful day. Happy to be alone to receive the applause of the house, the tenor did his best with the powers which have since achieved European fame. Genovese, then but three-and-twenty, born at Bergamo, a pupil of Veluti's and devoted to his art, a fine man, good-looking, clever in apprehending the spirit of a part, was already developing into the great artist destined to win fame and fortune. He had a wild success, - a phrase which is literally exact only in Italy, where the applause of the house is absolutely frenzied when a singer procures it enjoyment.

Some of the Prince's friends came to congratulate him on coming into his title, and to discuss the news. Only last evening la Tinti, taken by the Duke to the Vulpatos', had sung there, apparently in health as sound as her voice was fine; hence her sudden disposition gave rise to much comment. It was rumored at the Cafe Florian that Genovese was desperately in love with Clarina; that she was only anxious to avoid his declarations, and that the manager had tried in vain to induce her to appear with him. The Austrian General, on the other hand, asserted that it was the Duke who was ill, that the prima donna was nursing him, and that Genovese had been commanded to make amends to the public.

The Duchess owed this visit from the Austrian General to the fact that a French physician had come to Venice whom the General wished to introduce to her. The

Prince, seeing Vendramin wandering about the *parterre*, went out for a few minutes of confidential talk with his friend, whom he had not seen for three months; and as they walked round the gangway which divides the seats in the pit from the lowest tier of boxes, he had an opportunity of observing Massimilla's reception of the foreigner.

"Who is that Frenchman?" asked the Prince.

"A physician sent for by Cataneo, who wants to know how long he is likely to live," said Vendramin. "The Frenchman is waiting for Malfatti, with whom he is to hold a consultation."

Like every Italian woman who is in love, the Duchess kept her eyes fixed on Emilio; for in that land a woman is so wholly wrapped up in her lover that it is difficult to detect an expressive glance directed at anybody else.

"Caro," said the Prince to his friend, "remember I slept at your house last night."

"Have you triumphed?" said Vendramin, putting his arm round Emilio's waist.

"No; but I hope I may some day be happy with Massimilla."

"Well," replied Marco, "then you will be the most envied man on earth. The Duchess is the most perfect woman in Italy. To me, seeing things as I do through the dazzling medium of opium, she seems the very highest expression of art; for nature, without knowing it, has made her a Raphael picture. Your passion gives no umbrage to Cataneo, who has handed over to me a

Honore de Balzac

thousand crowns, which I am to give to you."

"Well," added Emilio, "whatever you may hear said, I sleep every night at your house. Come, for every minute spent away from her, when I might be with her, is torment."

Emilio took his seat at the back of the box and remained there in silence, listening to the Duchess, enchanted by her wit and beauty. It was for him, and not out of vanity, that Massimilla lavished the charms of her conversation bright with Italian wit, in which sarcasm lashed things but not persons, laughter attacked nothing that was not laughable, mere trifles were seasoned with Attic salt.

Anywhere else she might have been tiresome. The Italians, an eminently intelligent race, have no fancy for displaying their talents where they are not in demand; their chat is perfectly simple and effortless, it never makes play, as in France, under the lead of a fencing master, each one flourishing his foil, or, if he has nothing to say, sitting humiliated.

Conversation sparkles with a delicate and subtle satire that plays gracefully with familiar facts; and instead of a compromising epigram an Italian has a glance or a smile of unutterable meaning. They think - and they are right - that to be expected to understand ideas when they only seek enjoyment, is a bore.

Indeed, la Vulpato had said to Massimilla:

"If you loved him you would not talk so well."

Emilio took no part in the conversation; he listened and

gazed. This reserve might have led foreigners to suppose that the Prince was a man of no intelligence, - their impression very commonly of an Italian in love, - whereas he was simply a lover up to his ears in rapture. Vendramin sat down by Emilio, opposite the Frenchman, who, as the stranger, occupied the corner facing the Duchess.

"Is that gentleman drunk?" said the physician in an undertone to Massimilla, after looking at Vendramin.

"Yes," replied she, simply.

In that land of passion, each passion bears its excuse in itself, and gracious indulgence is shown to every form of error. The Duchess sighed deeply, and an expression of suppressed pain passed over her features.

"You will see strange things in our country, monsieur," she went on. "Vendramin lives on opium, as this one lives on love, and that one buries himself in learning; most young men have a passion for a dancer, as older men are miserly. We all create some happiness or some madness for ourselves."

"Because you all want to divert your minds from some fixed idea, for which a revolution would be a radical cure," replied the physician. "The Genoese regrets his republic, the Milanese pines for his independence, the Piemontese longs for a constitutional government, the Romagna cries for liberty -"

"Of which it knows nothing," interrupted the Duchess. "Alas! there are men in Italy so stupid as to long for your idiotic Charter, which destroys the influence of woman. Most of my fellow-countrywomen must need read your French books - useless rhodomontade -"

"Useless!" cried the Frenchman.

"Why, monsieur," the Duchess went on, "what can you find in a book that is better than what we have in our hearts? Italy is mad."

"I cannot see that a people is mad because it wishes to be its own master," said the physician.

"Good Heavens!" exclaimed the Duchess, eagerly, "does not that mean paying with a great deal of bloodshed for the right of quarreling, as you do, over crazy ideas?"

"Then you approve of despotism?" said the physician.

"Why should I not approve of a system of government which, by depriving us of books and odious politics, leaves men entirely to us?"

"I had thought that the Italians were more patriotic," said the Frenchman.

Massimilla laughed so slyly that her interlocutor could not distinguish mockery from serious meaning, nor her real opinion from ironical criticism.

"Then you are not a liberal?" said he.

"Heaven preserve me!" said she. "I can imagine nothing in worse taste than such opinions in a woman. Could you love a woman whose heart was occupied by all mankind?"

"Those who love are naturally aristocrats," the Austrian General observed, with a smile.

"As I came into the theatre," the Frenchman observed, "you were the first person I saw; and I remarked to his Excellency that if there was a woman who could personify a nation it was you. But I grieve to discover that, though you represent its divine beauty, you have not the constitutional spirit."

"Are you not bound," said the Duchess, pointing to the ballet now being danced, "to find all our dancers detestable and our singers atrocious? Paris and London rob us of all our leading stars. Paris passes judgment on them, and London pays them. Genovese and la Tinti will not be left to us for six months -"

At this juncture, the Austrian left the box. Vendramin, the Prince, and the other two Italians exchanged a look and a smile, glancing at the French physician. He, for a moment, felt doubtful of himself, - a rare thing in a Frenchman, - fancying he had said or done something incongruous; but the riddle was immediately solved.

"Do you thing it would be judicious," said Emilio, "if we spoke our mind in the presence of our masters?"

"You are in a land of slaves," said the Duchess, in a tone and with a droop of the head which gave her at once the look for which the physician had sought in vain. "Vendramin," she went on, speaking so that only the stranger could hear her, "took to smoking opium, a villainous idea suggested to him by an Englishman who, for other reasons of his, craved an easy death - not death as men see it in the form of a skeleton, but death draped with the frippery you in France call a flag

- a maiden form crowned with flowers or laurels; she appears in a cloud of gunpowder borne on the flight of a cannon-ball - or else stretched on a bed between two courtesans; or again, she rises in the steam of a bowl of punch, or the dazzling vapor of a diamond - but a diamond in the form of carbon.

"Whenever Vendramin chooses, for three Austrian lire, he can be a Venetian Captain, he can sail in the galleys of the Republic, and conquer the gilded domes of Constantinople. Then he can lounge on the divans in the Seraglio among the Sultan's wives, while the Grand Signor himself is the slave of the Venetian conqueror. He returns to restore his palazzo with the spoils of the Ottoman Empire. He can quit the women of the East for the doubly masked intrigues of his beloved Venetians, and fancy that he dreads the jealousy which has ceased to exist.

"For three zwanziger he can transport himself into the Council of Ten, can wield there terrible power, and leave the Doges' Palace to sleep under the watch of a pair of flashing eyes, or to climb a balcony from which a fair hand has hung a silken ladder. He can love a woman to whom opium lends such poetic grace as we women of flesh and blood could never show.

"Presently he turns over, and he is face to face with the dreadful frown of the senator, who holds a dagger. He hears the blade plunged into his mistress' heart. She dies smiling on him; for she has saved him.

"And she is a happy woman!" added the Duchess, looking at Emilio.

"He escapes and flies to command the Dalmatians, to

conquer the Illyrian coast for his beloved Venice. His glory wins him forgiveness, and he enjoys a life of domestic happiness, - a home, a winter evening, a young wife and charming children, who pray to San Marco under the care of an old nurse. Yes, for three francs' worth of opium he furnishes our empty arsenal, he watches convoys of merchandise coming in, going to the four quarters of the world. The forces of modern industry no longer reign in London, but in his own Venice, where the hanging gardens of Semiramis, the Temple of Jerusalem, the marvels of Rome, live once more. He adds to the glories of the middle ages by the labors of steam, by new masterpieces of art under the protection of Venice, who protected it of old. Monuments and nations crowd into his little brain; there is room for them all. Empires and cities and revolutions come and vanish in the course of a few hours, while Venice alone expands and lives; for the Venice of his dreams is the empress of the seas. She has two millions of inhabitants, the sceptre of Italy, the mastery of the Mediterranean and the Indies!"

"What an opera is the brain of man! What an unfathomed abyss! - even to those who, like Gall, have mapped it out," cried the physician.

"Dear Duchess," said Vendramin, "do not omit the last service that my elixir will do me. After hearing ravishing voices and imbibing music through every pore, after experiencing the keenest pleasures and the fiercest delights of Mahomet's paradise, I see none but the most terrible images. I have visions of my beloved Venice full of children's faces, distorted, like those of the dying; of women covered with dreadful wounds, torn and wailing; of men mangled and crushed by the copper sides of crashing vessels. I begin to see Venice as she is, shrouded in crape, stripped, robbed, destitute. Pale phantoms wander through her streets!

"Already the Austrian soldiers are grinning over me, already my visionary life is drifting into real life; whereas six months ago real life was the bad dream, and the life of opium held love and bliss, important affairs and political interests. Alas! To my grief, I see the dawn over my tomb, where truth and falsehood mingle in a dubious light, which is neither day nor darkness, but partakes of both."

"So you see that in this head there is too much patriotism," said the Prince, laying his hand on the thick black curls that fell on Vendramin's brow.

"Oh, if he loves us he will give up his dreadful opium!" said Massimilla.

"I will cure your friend," said the Frenchman.

"Achieve that, and we shall love you," said the Duchess. "But if on your return to France you do not calumniate us, we shall love you even better. The hapless Italians are too much crushed by foreign dominion to be fairly judged - for we have known yours," she added, with a smile.

"It was more generous than Austria's," said the physician, eagerly.

"Austria squeezes and gives us nothing back, and you squeeze to enlarge and beautify our towns; you stimulated us by giving us an army. You thought you could keep Italy, and they expect to lose it - there lies the difference.

"The Austrians provide us with a sort of ease that is as stultifying and heavy as themselves, while you overwhelmed us by your devouring energy. But whether we die of tonics or of narcotics, what does it matter? It is death all the same, Monsieur le docteur."

"Unhappy Italy! In my eyes she is like a beautiful woman whom France ought to protect by making her his mistress," exclaimed the Frenchman.

"But you could not love us as we wish to be loved," said the Duchess, smiling. "We want to be free. But the liberty I crave is not your ignoble and middle-class liberalism, which would kill all art. I ask," said she, in a tone that thrilled through the box, - "that is to say, I would ask, - that each Italian republic should be resuscitated, with its nobles, its citizens, its special privileges for each caste. I would have the old aristocratic republics once more with their intestine warfare and rivalry that gave birth to the noblest works of art, that created politics, that raised up the great princely houses. By extending the action of one government over a vast expanse of country it is frittered down. The Italian republics were the glory of Europe in the middle ages. Why has Italy succumbed when the Swiss, who were her porters, have triumphed?"

"The Swiss republics," said the doctor, "were worthy housewives, busy with their own little concerns, and neither having any cause for envying another. Your republics were haughty queens, preferring to sell themselves rather than bow to a neighbor; they fell too low ever to rise again. The Guelphs are triumphant."

"Do not pity us too much," said the Duchess, in a voice

that made the two friends start. "We are still supreme. Even in the depths of her misfortune Italy governs through the choicer spirits that abound in her cities.

"Unfortunately the greater number of her geniuses learn to understand life so quickly that they lie sunk in poverty-stricken pleasure. As for those who are willing to play the melancholy game for immortality, they know how to get at your gold and to secure your praises. Ay, in this land - pitied for its fallen state by traveled simpletons and hypocritical poets, while its character is traduced by politicians - in this land, which appears so languid, powerless, and ruinous, worn out rather than old, there are puissant brains in every branch of life, genius throwing out vigorous shoots as an old vine-stock throws out canes productive of delicious fruit. This race of ancient rulers still gives birth to kings - Lagrange, Volta, Rasori, Canova, Rossini, Bartolini, Galvani, Vigano, Beccaria, Cicognara, Corvetto. These Italians are masters of the scientific peaks on which they stand, or of the arts to which they devote themselves. To say nothing of the singers and executants who captivate Europe by their amazing perfections: Taglioni, Paganini, and the rest. Italy still rules the world which will always come to worship her.

"Go to Florian's to-night; you will find in Capraja one of our cleverest men, but in love with obscurity. No one but the Duke, my master, understands music so thoroughly as he does; indeed he is known here as *il Fanatico*."

After sitting a few minutes listening to the eager war of words between the physician and the Duchess, who showed much ingenious eloquence, the Italians, one by one, took leave, and went off to tell the news in every box, that la Cataneo, who was regarded as a woman of great wit and spirit, had, on the question of Italy, defeated a famous French doctor. This was the talk of the evening.

As soon as the Frenchman found himself alone with the Duchess and the Prince, he understood that they were to be left together, and took leave. Massimilla bowed with a bend of the neck that placed him at such a distance that this salute might have secured her the man's hatred, if he could have ignored the charm of her eloquence and beauty.

Thus at the end of the opera, Emilio and Massimilla were alone, and holding hands they listened together to the duet that finishes *Il Barbiere*.

"There is nothing but music to express love," said the Duchess, moved by that song as of two rapturous nightingales.

A tear twinkled in Emilio's eye; Massimilla, sublime in such beauty as beams in Raphael's Saint-Cecilia, pressed his hand, their knees touched, there was, as it seemed, the blossom of a kiss on her lips. The Prince saw on her blushing face a glow of joy like that which on a summer's day shines down on the golden harvest; his heart seemed bursting with the tide of blood that rushed to it. He fancied that he could hear an angelic chorus of voices, and he would have given his life to feel the fire of passion which at this hour last night had filled him for the odious Clarina; but he was at the moment hardly conscious of having a body.

Massimilla, much distressed, ascribed this tear, in her

guilelessness, to the remark she had made as to Genovese's cavatina.

"But, *carino*," said she in Emilio's ear, "are not you as far better than every expression of love, as cause is superior to effect?"

After handing the Duchess to her gondola, Emilio waited for Vendramin to go to Florian's.

The Cafe Florian at Venice is a quite undefinable institution. Merchants transact their business there, and lawyers meet to talk over their most difficult cases. Florian's is at once an Exchange, a green-room, a newspaper office, a club, a confessional, - and it is so well adapted to the needs of the place that some Venetian women never know what their husband's business may be, for, if they have a letter to write, they go to write it there.

Spies, of course, abound at Florian's; but their presence only sharpens Venetian wits, which may here exercise the discretion once so famous. A great many persons spend the whole day at Florian's; in fact, to some men Florian's is so much a matter of necessity, that between the acts of an opera they leave the ladies in their boxes and take a turn to hear what is going on there.

While the two friends were walking in the narrow streets of the Merceria they did not speak, for there were too many people; but as they turned into the Piazzi di San Marco, the Prince said:

"Do not go at once to the cafe. Let us walk about; I want to talk to you."

He related his adventure with Clarina and explained his position. To Vendramin Emilio's despair seemed so nearly allied to madness that he promised to cure him completely if only he would give him *carte blanche* to deal with Massimilla. This ray of hope came just in time to save Emilio from drowning himself that night; for, indeed, as he remembered the singer, he felt a horrible wish to go back to her.

The two friends then went to an inner room at Florian's, where they listened to the conversation of some of the superior men of the town, who discoursed the subjects of the day. The most interesting of these were, in the first place, the eccentricities of Lord Byron, of whom the Venetians made great sport; then Cataneo's attachment for la Tinti, for which no reason could be assigned after twenty different causes had been suggested; then Genovese's debut; finally, the tilting match between the Duchess and the French doctor. Just as the discussion became vehemently musical, Duke Cataneo made his appearance. He bowed very courteously to Emilio, which seemed so natural that no one noticed it, and Emilio bowed gravely in return. Cataneo looked round to see if there was anybody he knew, recognized Vendramin and greeted him, bowed to his banker, a rich patrician, and finally to the man who happened to be speaking, - a celebrated musical fanatic, a friend of the Comtesse Albrizzi. Like some others who frequented Florian's, his mode of life was absolutely unknown, so carefully did he conceal it. Nothing was known about him but what he chose to tell.

This was Capraja, the nobleman whom the Duchess had mentioned to the French doctor. This Venetian was one of a class of dreamers whose powerful minds divine everything. He was an eccentric theorist, and cared no more for celebrity than for a broken pipe.

His life was in accordance with his ideas. Capraja made his appearance at about ten every morning under the *Procuratie*, without anyone knowing whence he came. He lounged about Venice, smoking cigars. He regularly went to the Fenice, sitting in the pit-stalls, and between the acts went round to Florian's, where he took three or four cups of coffee a day; and he ended the evening at the cafe, never leaving it till about two in the morning. Twelve hundred francs a year paid all his expenses; he ate but one meal a day at an eating-house in the Merceria, where the cook had his dinner ready for him at a fixed hour, on a little table at the back of the shop; the pastry-cook's daughter herself prepared his stuffed oysters, provided him with cigars, and took care of his money. By his advice, this girl, though she was very handsome, would never countenance a lover, lived very steadily, and still wore the old Venetian costume. This purely-bred Venetian girl was twelve years old when Capraja first took an interest in her, and six-and-twenty when he died. She was very fond of him, though he had never even kissed her hand or her brow, and she knew nothing whatever of the poor old nobleman's intentions with regard to her. The girl had at last as complete control of the old gentle-man as a mother has of her child; she would tell him when he wanted clean linen; next day he would come without a shirt, and she would give him a clean one to put on in the morning.

He never looked at a woman either in the theatre or out walking. Though he was the descendant of an old patrician family he never thought his rank worth mentioning. But at night, after twelve, he awoke from his apathy, talked, and showed that he had seen and heard everything. This peaceful Diogenes, quite incapable of explaining his tenets, half a Turk, half a Venetian, was thick-set, short, and fat; he had a Doge's sharp nose, an inquisitive, satirical eye, and a discreet though smiling mouth.

When he died, it became known that he had lived in a little den near San Benedetto. He had two million francs invested in the funds of various countries of Europe, and had left the interest untouched ever since he had first bought the securities in 1814, so the sum was now enormous, alike from the increased value of the capital and the accumulated interest. All this money was left to the pastry-cook's daughter.

"Genovese," he was saying, "will do wonders. Whether he really understands the great end of music, or acts only on instinct, I know not; but he is the first singer who ever satisfied me. I shall not die without hearing a *cadenza* executed as I have heard them in my dreams, waking with a feeling as though the sounds were floating in the air. The clear *cadenza* is the highest achievement of art; it is the arabesque, decorating the finest room in the house; a shade too little and it is nothing, a touch too much and all is confusion. Its task is to awake in the soul a thousand dormant ideas; it flies up and sweeps through space, scattering seeds in the air to be taken in by our ears and blossom in our heart. Believe me, in painting his Saint-Cecilia, Raphael gave the preference to music over poetry. And he was right; music appeals to the heart, whereas writing is addressed to the intellect; it communicates ideas directly, like a perfume. The singer's voice impinges not on the mind, not on the memory of happiness, but on the first principle of thought; it stirs the elements of sensation.

"It is a grievous thing that the populace should have compelled musicians to adapt their expression to words, to factitious emotions; but then they were not otherwise intelligible to the vulgar. Thus the *cadenza* is the only thing left to the lovers of pure music, the devotees of unfettered art. To-night, as I listened to that last *cavatina*, I felt as if I were beckoned by a fair creature whose look alone had made me young again. The enchantress placed a crown on my brow, and led me to the ivory door through which we pass to the mysterious land of day-dreams. I owe it to Genovese that I escaped for a few minutes from this old husk - minutes, short no doubt by the clock, but very long by the record of sensation. For a brief spring-time, scented with roses, I was young again - and beloved!"

"But you are mistaken, *caro* Capraja," said the Duke. "There is in music an effect yet more magical than that of the *cadenza*."

"What is that?" asked Capraja.

"The unison of two voices, or of a voice and a violin, - the instrument which has tones most nearly resembling those of the human voice," replied Cataneo. "This perfect concord bears us on to the very heart of life, on the tide of elements which can resuscitate rapture and carry man up to the centre of the luminous sphere where his mind can command the whole universe. You still need a *thema*, Capraja, but the pure element is enough for me. You need that the current should flow through the myriad canals of the machine to fall in dazzling cascades, while I am content with the pure tranquil pool. My eye gazes across a lake without a ripple. I can embrace the infinite."

"Speak no more, Cataneo," said Capraja, haughtily. "What! Do you fail to see the fairy, who, in her swift rush through the sparkling atmosphere, collects and binds with the golden thread of harmony, the gems of melody she smilingly sheds on us? Have you ever felt the touch of her wand, as she says to Curiosity, 'Awake!' The divinity rises up radiant from the depths of the brain; she flies to her store of wonders and fingers them lightly as an organist touches the keys. Suddenly, up starts Memory, bringing us the roses of the past, divinely preserved and still fresh. The mistress of our youth revives, and strokes the young man's hair. Our heart, too full, overflows; we see the flowery banks of the torrent of love. Every burning bush we ever knew blazes afresh, and repeats the heavenly words we once heard and understood. The voice rolls on; it embraces in its rapid turns those fugitive horizons, and they shrink away; they vanish, eclipsed by newer and deeper joys - those of an unrevealed future, to which the fairy points as she returns to the blue heaven."

"And you," retorted Cataneo, "have you never seen the direct ray of a star opening the vistas above; have you never mounted on that beam which guides you to the sky, to the heart of the first causes which move the worlds?"

To their hearers, the Duke and Capraja were playing a game of which the premises were unknown.

"Genovese's voice thrills through every fibre," said Capraja.

"And la Tinti's fires the blood," replied the Duke.

"What a paraphrase of happy love is that *cavatina*!" Capraja went on. "Ah! Rossini was young when he wrote that interpretation of effervescent ecstasy. My heart filled with renewed blood, a thousand cravings tingled in my veins. Never have sounds more angelic delivered me more completely from my earthly bonds! Never did the fairy wave more beautiful arms, smile more invitingly, lift her tunic more cunningly to display an ankle, raising the curtain that hides my other life!"

"To-morrow, my old friend," replied Cataneo, "you shall ride on the back of a dazzling, white swan, who will show you the loveliest land there is; you shall see the spring-time as children see it. Your heart shall open to the radiance of a new sun; you shall sleep on crimson silk, under the gaze of a Madonna; you shall feel like a happy lover gently kissed by a nymph whose bare feet you still may see, but who is about to vanish. That swan will be the voice of Genovese, if he can unite it to its Leda, the voice of Clarina. To-morrow night we are to hear *Mose*, the grandest opera produced by Italy's greatest genius."

All present left the conversation to the Duke and Capraja, not wishing to be the victims of mystification. Only Vendramin and the French doctor listened to them for a few minutes. The opium-smoker understood these poetic flights; he had the key of the palace where those two sensuous imaginations were wandering. The doctor, too, tried to understand, and he understood, for he was one of the Pleiades of genius belonging to the Paris school of medicine, from which a true physician comes out as much a metaphysician as an accomplished analyst.

"Do you understand them?" said Emilio to Vendramin as they left the cafe at two in the morning.

"Yes, my dear boy," said Vendramin, taking Emilio home with him. "Those two men are of the legion of unearthly spirits to whom it is given here below to escape from the wrappings of the flesh, who can fly on the shoulders of the queen of witchcraft up to the blue empyrean where the sublime marvels are wrought of the intellectual life; they, by the power of art, can soar whither your immense love carries you, whither opium transports me. Then none can understand them but those who are like them.

"I, who can inspire my soul by such base means, who can pack a hundred years of life into a single night, I can understand those lofty spirits when they talk of that glorious land, deemed a realm of chimeras by some who think themselves wise; but the realm of reality to us whom they think mad. Well, the Duke and Capraja, who were acquainted at Naples, - where Cataneo was born, - are mad about music."

"But what is that strange system that Capraja was eager to explain to the Duke? Did you understand?"

"Yes," replied Vendramin. "Capraja's great friend is a musician from Cremona, lodging in the Capello palace, who has a theory that sounds meet with an element in man, analogous to that which produces ideas. According to him, man has within him keys acted on by sound, and corresponding to his nerve-centres, where ideas and sensations take their rise. Capraja, who regards the arts as an assemblage of means by which he can harmonize, in himself, all external nature with another mysterious nature that he calls the inner life, shares all ideas of this instrument-maker, who at this moment is composing an opera.

"Conceive of a sublime creation, wherein the marvels of the visible universe are reproduced with immeasurable grandeur, lightness, swiftness, and extension; wherein sensation is infinite, and whither certain privileged natures, possessed of divine powers, are able to penetrate, and you will have some notion of the ecstatic joys of which Cataneo and Capraja were speaking; both poets, each for himself alone. Only, in matters of the intellect, as soon as a man can rise above the sphere where plastic art is produced by a process of imitation, and enter into that transcendental sphere of abstractions where everything is understood as an elementary principle, and seen in the omnipotence of results, that man is no longer intelligible to ordinary minds."

"You have thus explained my love for Massimilla," said Emilio. "There is in me, my friend, a force which awakes under the fire of her look, at her lightest touch, and wafts me to a world of light where effects are produced of which I dare not speak. It has seemed to me often that the delicate tissue of her skin has stamped flowers on mine as her hand lies on my hand. Her words play on those inner keys in me, of which you spoke. Desire excites my brain, stirring that invisible world, instead of exciting my passive flesh; the air seems red and sparkling, unknown perfumes of indescribable strength relax my sinews, roses wreathe my temples, and I feel as though my blood were escaping through opened arteries, so complete is my inanition."

"That is the effect on me of smoking opium," replied Vendramin.

"Then do you wish to die?" cried Emilio, in alarm.

"With Venice!" said Vendramin, waving his hand in the direction of San Marco. "Can you see a single pinnacle or spire that stands straight? Do you not perceive that the sea is claiming its prey?"

The Prince bent his head; he dared no more speak to his friend of love.

To know what a free country means, you must have traveled in a conquered land.

When they reached the Palazzo Vendramin, they saw a gondola moored at the water-gate. The Prince put his arm round Vendramin and clasped him affectionately, saying:

"Good-night to you, my dear fellow!"

"What! a woman? for me, whose only love is Venice?" exclaimed Marco.

At this instant the gondolier, who was leaning against a column, recognizing the man he was to look out for, murmured in Emilio's ear:

"The Duchess, monseigneur."

Emilio sprang into the gondola, where he was seized in a pair of soft arms - an embrace of iron - and dragged down on to the cushions, where he felt the heaving bosom of an ardent woman. And then he was no more

Emilio, but Clarina's lover; for his ideas and feelings were so bewildering that he yielded as if stupefied by her first kiss.

"Forgive this trick, my beloved," said the Sicilian. "I shall die if you do not come with me."

And the gondola flew over the secret water.

At half-past seven on the following evening, the spectators were again in their places in the theatre, excepting that those in the pit always took their chances of where they might sit. Old Capraja was in Cataneo's box.

Before the overture the Duke paid a call on the Duchess; he made a point of standing behind her and leaving the front seat to Emilio next the Duchess. He made a few trivial remarks, without sarcasm or bitterness, and with as polite a manner as if he were visiting a stranger.

But in spite of his efforts to seem amiable and natural, the Prince could not control his expression, which was deeply anxious. Bystanders would have ascribed such a change in his usually placid features to jealousy. The Duchess no doubt shared Emilio's feelings; she looked gloomy and was evidently depressed. The Duke, uncomfortable enough between two sulky people, took advantage of the French doctor's entrance to slip away.

"Monsieur," said Cataneo to his physician before dropping the curtain over the entrance to the box, "you will hear to-night a grand musical poem, not easy of comprehension at a first hearing. But in leaving you with the Duchess I know that you can have no more competent interpreter, for she is my pupil."

The doctor, like the Duke, was struck by the expression stamped on the faces of the lovers, a look of pining despair.

"Then does an Italian opera need a guide to it?" he asked Massimilla, with a smile.

Recalled by this question to her duties as mistress of the box, the Duchess tried to chase away the clouds that darkened her brow, and replied, with eager haste, to open a conversation in which she might vent her irritation: -

"This is not so much an opera, monsieur," said she, "as an oratorio - a work which is in fact not unlike a most magnificent edifice, and I shall with pleasure be your guide. Believe me, it will not be too much to give all your mind to our great Rossini, for you need to be at once a poet and a musician to appreciate the whole bearing of such a work.

"You belong to a race whose language and genius are too practical for it to enter into music without an effort; but France is too intellectual not to learn to love it and cultivate it, and to succeed in that as in everything else. Also, it must be acknowledged that music, as created by Lulli, Rameau, Haydn, Mozart, Beethoven, Cimarosa, Paisiello, and Rossini, and as it will be carried on by the great geniuses of the future, is a new art, unknown to former generations; they had indeed no such variety of instruments on which the flowers of melody now blossom as on some rich soil.

"So novel an art demands study in the public, study of

a kind that may develop the feelings to which music appeals. That sentiment hardly exists as yet among you - a nation given up to philosophical theories, to analysis and discussion, and always torn by civil disturbances. Modern music demands perfect peace; it is the language of loving and sentimental souls, inclined to lofty emotional aspiration.

"That language, a thousand times fuller than the language of words, is to speech and ideas what the thought is to its utterance; it arouses sensations and ideas in their primitive form, in that part of us where sensations and ideas have their birth, but leaves them as they are in each of us. That power over our inmost being is one of the grandest facts in music. All other arts present to the mind a definite creation; those of music are indefinite - infinite. We are compelled to accept the ideas of the poet, the painter's picture, the sculptor's statue; but music each one can interpret at the will of his sorrow or his gladness, his hope or his despair. While other arts restrict our mind by fixing it on a predestined object, music frees it to roam over all nature which it alone has the power of expressing. You shall hear how I interpret Rossini's *Mose*."

She leaned across to the Frenchman to speak to him, without being overheard.

"Moses is the liberator of an enslaved race!" said she. "Remember that, and you will see with what religious hope the whole house will listen to the prayer of the rescued Hebrews, with what a thunder of applause it will respond!"

As the leader raised his bow, Emilio flung himself into a back seat. The Duchess pointed out the place he had left, for the physician to take it. But the Frenchman was far more curious to know what had gone wrong between the lovers than to enter the halls of music built up by the man whom all Italy was applauding - for it was the day of Rossini's triumph in his own country. He was watching the Duchess, and she was talking with a feverish excitement. She reminded him of the Niobe he had admired at Florence: the same dignity in woe, the same physical control; and yet her soul shone though, in the warm flush of her cheeks; and her eyes, where anxiety was disguised under a flash of pride, seemed to scorch the tears away by their fire. Her suppressed grief seemed calmer when she looked at Emilio, who never took his eyes off her; it was easy to see that she was trying to mollify some fierce despair. The state of her feelings gave a certain loftiness to her mind.

Like most women when under the stress of some unusual agitation, she overstepped her ordinary limitations and assumed something of the Pythoness, though still remaining calm and beautiful; for it was the form of her thoughts that was wrung with desperation, not the features of her face. And perhaps she wanted to shine with all her wit to lend some charm to life and detain her lover from death.

When the orchestra had given out the three chords in C major, placed at the opening by the composer to announce that the overture will be sung - for the real overture is the great movement beginning with this stern attack, and ending only when light appears at the command of Moses - the Duchess could not control a little spasmodic start, that showed how entirely the music was in accordance with her concealed distress.

"Those three chords freeze the blood," said she. "They announce trouble. Listen attentively to this introduction; the terrible lament of a nation stricken by the hand of God. What wailing! The King, the Queen, their first-born son, all the dignitaries of the kingdom are sighing; they are wounded in their pride, in their conquests; checked in their avarice. Dear Rossini! you have done well to throw this bone to gnaw to the *Tedeschi*, who declared we had no harmony, no science!

"Now you will hear the ominous melody the maestro has engrafted on to this profound harmonic composition, worthy to compare with the most elaborate structures of the Germans, but never fatiguing or tiresome.

"You French, who carried through such a bloodthirsty revolution, who crushed your aristocracy under the paw of the lion mob, on the day when this oratorio is performed in your capital, you will understand this glorious dirge of the victims on whom God is avenging his chosen people. None but an Italian could have written this pregnant and inexhaustible theme - truly Dantesque. Do you think that it is nothing to have such a dream of vengeance, even for a moment? Handel, Sebastian Bach, all you old German masters, nay, even you, great Beethoven, on your knees! Here is the queen of arts, Italy triumphant!"

The Duchess had spoken while the curtain was being raised. And now the physician heard the sublime symphony with which the composer introduces the great Biblical drama. It is to express the sufferings of a whole nation. Suffering is uniform in its expression, especially physical suffering. Thus, having instinctively felt, like all men of genius, that here there must be no variety of idea, the musician, having hit on his leading phrase, has worked it out in various keys, grouping the masses and the dramatis personae to take up the theme through modulations and cadences of admirable structure. In such simplicity is power.

"The effect of this strain, depicting the sensations of night and cold in a people accustomed to live in the bright rays of the sun, and sung by the people and their princes, is most impressive. There is something relentless in that slow phrase of music; it is cold and sinister, like an iron bar wielded by some celestial executioner, and dropping in regular rhythm on the limbs of all his victims. As we hear it passing from C minor into G minor, returning to C and again to the dominant G, starting afresh and *fortissimo* on the tonic B flat, drifting into F major and back to C minor, and in each key in turn more ominously terrible, chill, and dark, we are compelled at last to enter into the impression intended by the composer."

The Frenchman was, in fact, deeply moved when all this united sorrow exploded in the cry:

"O Nume d'Israel,
Se brami in liberta
Il popol tuo fedel,
Di lui di noi pieta!"

(O God of Israel, if thou wouldst see thy faithful people free, have mercy on them, and on us.)

"Never was a grander synthesis composed of natural effects or a more perfect idealization of nature. In a great national disaster, each one for a long time bewails himself alone; then, from out of the mass, rises up, here and there, a more emphatic and vehement cry of anguish; finally, when the misery has fallen on all, it bursts forth like a tempest.

"As soon as they all recognize a common grievance, the dull murmurs of the people become cries of impatience. Rossini has proceeded on this hypothesis. After the outcry in C major, Pharoah sings his grand recitative: *Mano ultrice di un Dio* (Avenging hand of God), after which the original subject is repeated with more vehement expression. All Egypt appeals to Moses for help."

The Duchess had taken advantage of the pause for the entrance of Moses and Aaron to give this interpretation of that fine introduction.

"Let them weep!" she added passionately. "They have done much ill. Expiate your sins, Egyptians, expiate the crimes of your maddened Court! With what amazing skill has this great painter made use of all the gloomy tones of music, of all that is saddest on the musical palette! What creepy darkness! what a mist! Is not your very spirit in mourning? Are you not convinced of the reality of the blackness that lies over the land? Do you not feel that Nature is wrapped in the deepest shades? There are no palm-trees, no Egyptian palaces, no landscape. And what a healing to your soul will the deeply religious strain be of the heaven-sent Healer who will stay this cruel plague! How skilfully is everything wrought up to end in that glorious invocation of Moses to God.

"By a learned elaboration, which Capraja could explain to you, this appeal to heaven is accompanied by brass instruments only; it is that which gives it such a solemn, religious cast. And not merely is the artifice fine in its place; note how fertile in resource is genius. Rossini has derived fresh beauty from the difficulty he himself created. He has the strings in reserve to express daylight when it succeeds to the darkness, and thus produces one of the greatest effects ever achieved in music.

"Till this inimitable genius showed the way never was such a result obtained with mere *recitative*. We have not, so far, had an air or a duet. The poet has relied on the strength of the idea, on the vividness of his imagery, and the realism of the declamatory passages. This scene of despair, this darkness that may be felt, these cries of anguish, - the whole musical picture is as fine as your great Poussin's *Deluge*."

Moses waved his staff, and it was light.

"Here, monsieur, does not the music vie with the sun, whose splendor it has borrowed, with nature, whose phenomena it expresses in every detail?" the Duchess went on, in an undertone. "Art here reaches its climax; no musician can get beyond this. Do not you hear Egypt waking up after its long torpor? Joy comes in with the day. In what composition, ancient or modern, will you find so grand a passage? The greatest gladness in contrast to the deepest woe! What exclamations! What gleeful notes! The oppressed spirit breathes again. What delirium in the *tremolo* of the orchestra! What a noble *tutti*! This is the rejoicing of a delivered nation. Are you not thrilled with joy?"

The physician, startled by the contrast, was, in fact, clapping his hands, carried away by admiration for one of the finest compositions of modern music.

"*Brava la Doni!*" said Vendramin, who had heard the Duchess.

"Now the introduction is ended," said she. "You have gone through a great sensation," she added, turning to the Frenchman. "Your heart is beating; in the depths of your imagination you have a splendid sunrise, flooding with light a whole country that before was cold and dark. Now, would you know the means by which the musician has worked, so as to admire him to-morrow for the secrets of his craft after enjoying the results to-night? What do you suppose produces this effect of daylight - so sudden, so complicated, and so complete? It consists of a simple chord of C, constantly reiterated, varied only by the chord of 4-6. This reveals the magic of his touch. To show you the glory of light he has worked by the same means that he used to represent darkness and sorrow.

"This dawn in imagery is, in fact, absolutely the same as the natural dawn; for light is one and the same thing everywhere, always alike in itself, the effects varying only with the objects it falls on. Is it not so? Well, the musician has taken for the fundamental basis of his music, for its sole *motif*, a simple chord in C. The sun first sheds its light on the mountain-tops and then in the valleys. In the same way the chord is first heard on the treble string of the violins with boreal mildness; it spreads through the orchestra, it awakes the instruments one by one, and flows among them. Just as light glides from one thing to the next, giving them color, the music moves on, calling out each rill of harmony till all flow together in the *tutti*.

"The violins, silent until now, give the signal with their tender *tremolo*, softly *agitato* like the first rays of morning. That light, cheerful movement, which caresses the soul, is cleverly supported by chords in the bass, and by a vague *fanfare* on the trumpets, restricted to their lowest notes, so as to give a vivid idea of the last cool shadows that linger in the valleys while the first warm rays touch the heights. Then all the wind is gradually added to strengthen the general harmony. The voices come in with sighs of delight and surprise. At last the brass breaks out, the trumpets sound. Light, the source of all harmony, inundates all nature; every musical resource is produced with a turbulence, a splendor, to compare with that of the Eastern sun. Even the triangle, with its reiterated C, reminds us by its shrill accent and playful rhythm of the song of early birds.

"Thus the same key, freshly treated by the master's hand, expresses the joy of all nature, while it soothes the grief it uttered before.

"There is the hall-mark of the great genius: Unity. It is the same but different. In one and the same phrase we find a thousand various feelings of woe, the misery of a nation. In one and the same chord we have all the various incidents of awakening nature, every expression of the nation's joy. These two tremendous passages are soldered into one by the prayer to an ever-living God, author of all things, of that woe and that gladness alike. Now is not that introduction by itself a grand poem?"

"It is, indeed," said the Frenchman.

"Next comes a quintette such as Rossini can give us. If

he was ever justified in giving vent to that flowery, voluptuous grace for which Italian music is blamed, is it not in this charming movement in which each person expresses joy? The enslaved people are delivered, and yet a passion in peril is fain to moan. Pharaoh's son loves a Hebrew woman, and she must leave him. What gives its ravishing charm to this quintette is the return to the homelier feelings of life after the grandiose picture of two stupendous and national emotions: - general misery, general joy, expressed with the magic force stamped on them by divine vengeance and with the miraculous atmosphere of the Bible narrative. Now, was not I right?" added Massimilla, as the noble *sretto* came to a close.

"Voci di giubilo,
D' in'orno eccheggino,
Di pace l' Iride
Per noi spunto."

(Cries of joy sound about us. The rainbow of peace dawns upon us.)

"How ingeniously the composer has constructed this passage!" she went on, after waiting for a reply. "He begins with a solo on the horn, of divine sweetness, supported by *arpeggios* on the harps; for the first voices to be heard in this grand concerted piece are those of Moses and Aaron returning thanks to the true God. Their strain, soft and solemn, reverts to the sublime ideas of the invocation, and mingles, nevertheless, with the joy of the heathen people. This transition combines the heavenly and the earthly in a way which genius alone could invent, giving the *andante* of this quintette a glow of color that I can only compare to the light thrown by Titian on his Divine Persons. Did you observe the exquisite interweaving of the voices? the clever entrances by which the composer has grouped them round the main idea given out by the orchestra? the learned progressions that prepare us for the festal *allegro*? Did you not get a glimpse, as it were, of dancing groups, the dizzy round of a whole nation escaped from danger? And when the clarionet gives the signal for the *stretto*, - '*Voci di giubilo*,' - so brilliant and gay, was not your soul filled with the sacred pyrrhic joy of which David speaks in the Psalms, ascribing it to the hills?"

"Yes, it would make a delightful dance tune," said the doctor.

"French! French! always French!" exclaimed the Duchess, checked in her exultant mood by this sharp thrust. "Yes; you would be capable of taking that wonderful burst of noble and dainty rejoicing and turning it into a rigadoon. Sublime poetry finds no mercy in your eyes. The highest genius, - saints, kings, disasters, - all that is most sacred must pass under the rods of caricature. And the vulgarizing of great music by turning it into a dance tune is to caricature it. With you, wit kills soul, as argument kills reason."

They all sat in silence through the *recitative* of Osiride and Membrea, who plot to annul the order given by Pharaoh for the departure of the Hebrews.

"Have I vexed you?" asked the physician to the Duchess. "I should be in despair. Your words are like a magic wand. They unlock the pigeon-holes of my brain, and let out new ideas, vivified by this sublime music."

"No," replied she, "you have praised our great composer after your own fashion. Rossini will be a success with you, for the sake of his witty and sensual gifts. Let us hope that he may find some noble souls, in love with the ideal - which must exist in your fruitful land, - to appreciate the sublimity, the loftiness, of such music. Ah, now we have the famous duet, between Elcia and Osiride!" she exclaimed, and she went on, taking advantage of the triple salvo of applause which hailed la Tinti, as she made her first appearance on the stage.

"If la Tinti has fully understood the part of Elcia, you will hear the frenzied song of a woman torn by her love for her people, and her passion for one of their oppressors, while Osiride, full of mad adoration for his beautiful vassal, tries to detain her. The opera is built up as much on that grand idea as on that of Pharaoh's resistance to the power of God and of liberty; you must enter into it thoroughly or you will not understand this stupendous work.

"Notwithstanding the disfavor you show to the dramas invented by our *libretto* writers, you must allow me to point out the skill with which this one is constructed. The antithesis required in every fine work, and eminently favorable to music, is well worked out. What can be finer than a whole nation demanding liberty, held in bondage by bad faith, upheld by God, and piling marvel on marvel to gain freedom? What more dramatic than the Prince's love for a Hebrew woman, almost justifying treason to the oppressor's power?

"And this is what is expressed in this bold and stupendous musical poem; Rossini has stamped each nation with its fantastic individuality, for we have attributed to them a certain historic grandeur to which every imagination subscribes. The songs of the Hebrews, and their trust in God, are perpetually contrasted with Pharaoh's shrieks of rage and vain efforts, represented with a strong hand.

"At this moment Osiride, thinking only of love, hopes to detain his mistress by the memories of their joys as lovers; he wants to conquer the attractions of her feeling for her people. Here, then, you will find delicious languor, the glowing sweetness, the voluptuous suggestions of Oriental love, in the air '*Ah! se puoi cosi lasciarmi*,' sung by Osiride, and in Elcia's reply, '*Ma perche cosi straziarmi?*' No; two hearts in such melodious unison could never part," she went on, looking at the Prince.

"But the lovers are suddenly interrupted by the exultant voice of the Hebrew people in the distance, which recalls Elcia. What a delightful and inspiriting *allegro* is the theme of this march, as the Israelites set out for the desert! No one but Rossini can make wind instruments and trumpets say so much. And is not the art which can express in two phrases all that is meant by the 'native land' certainly nearer to heaven than the others? This clarion-call always moves me so deeply that I cannot find words to tell you how cruel it is to an enslaved people to see those who are free march away!"

The Duchess' eyes filled with tears as she listened to the grand movement, which in fact crowns the opera.

"*Dov' e mai quel core amante*," she murmured in Italian, as la Tinti began the delightful *aria* of the *stretto* in which she implores pity for her grief. "But what is the matter? The pit are dissatisfied -"

"Genovese is braying like a stage," replied the Prince.

In point of fact, this first duet with la Tinti was spoilt by Genovese's utter breakdown. His excellent method, recalling that of Crescentini and Veluti, seemed to desert him completely. A *sostenuto* in the wrong place, an embellishment carried to excess, spoilt the effect; or again a loud climax with no due *crescendo*, an outburst of sound like water tumbling through a suddenly opened sluice, showed complete and wilful neglect of the laws of good taste.

The pit was in the greatest excitement. The Venetian public believed there was a deliberate plot between Genovese and his friends. La Tinti was recalled and applauded with frenzy while Genovese had a hint or two warning him of the hostile feeling of the audience. During this scene, highly amusing to a Frenchman, while la Tinti was recalled eleven times to receive alone the frantic acclamations of the house, - Genovese, who was all but hissed, not daring to offer her his hand, - the doctor made a remark to the Duchess as to the *stretto* of the duet.

"In this place," said he, "Rossini ought to have expressed the deepest grief, and I find on the contrary an airy movement, a tone of ill-timed cheerfulness."

"You are right," said she. "This mistake is the result of a tyrannous custom which composers are expected to obey. He was thinking more of his prima donna than of Elcia when he wrote that *stretto*. But this evening, even if la Tinti had been more brilliant than ever, I could throw myself so completely into the situation, that the passage, lively as it is, is to me full of sadness."

The physician looked attentively from the Prince to the Duchess, but could not guess the reason that held them apart, and that made this duet seem to them so heartrending.

"Now comes a magnificent thing, the scheming of Pharaoh against the Hebrews. The great *aria 'A rispettarmi apprenda'* (Learn to respect me) is a triumph for Carthagenova, who will express superbly the offended pride and the duplicity of a sovereign. The Throne will speak. He will withdraw the concessions that have been made, he arms himself in wrath. Pharaoh rises to his feet to clutch the prey that is escaping.

"Rossini never wrote anything grander in style, or stamped with more living and irresistible energy. It is a consummate work, supported by an accompaniment of marvelous orchestration, as indeed is every portion of this opera. The vigor of youth illumines the smallest details."

The whole house applauded this noble movement, which was admirably rendered by the singer, and thoroughly appreciated by the Venetians.

"In the *finale*," said the Duchess, "you hear a repetition of the march, expressive of the joy of deliverance and of faith in God, who allows His people to rush off gleefully to wander in the Desert! What lungs but would be refreshed by the aspirations of a whole nation freed from slavery.

"Oh, beloved and living melodies! Glory to the great genius who has known how to give utterance to such feelings! There is something essentially warlike in that march, proclaiming that the God of armies is on the side of these people. How full of feeling are these strains of thanksgiving! The imagery of the Bible rises up in our mind; this glorious musical *scena* enables us to realize one of the grandest dramas of that ancient and solemn world. The religious form given to some of the voice parts, and the way in which they come in, one by one, to group with the others, express all we have ever imagined of the sacred marvels of that early age of humanity.

"And yet this fine concerted piece is no more than a development of the theme of the march into all its musical outcome. That theme is the inspiring element alike for the orchestra and the voices, for the air, and for the brilliant instrumentation that supports it.

"Elcia now comes to join the crowd; and to give shade to the rejoicing spirit of this number, Rossini has made her utter her regrets. Listen to her *duettino* with Amenofi. Did blighted love ever express itself in lovelier song? It is full of the grace of a *notturno*, of the secret grief of hopeless love. How sad! how sad! The Desert will indeed be a desert to her!

"After this comes the fierce conflict of the Egyptians and the Hebrews. All their joy is spoiled, their march stopped by the arrival of the Egyptians. Pharaoh's edict is proclaimed in a musical phrase, hollow and dread, which is the leading *motif* of the *finale*; we could fancy that we hear the tramp of the great Egyptian army, surrounding the sacred phalanx of the true God, curling round it, like a long African serpent enveloping its prey. But how beautiful is the lament of the duped and disappointed Hebrews! Though, in truth, it is more Italian than Hebrew. What a superb passage introduces Pharaoh's arrival, when his presence brings the two leaders face to face, and all the moving passions of the drama. The conflict of sentiments in that sublime *ottetto*, where the wrath of Moses meets that of the two Pharaohs, is admirable. What a medley of voices and of unchained furies!

"No grander subject was ever wrought out by a composer. The famous *finale* of *Don Giovanni*, after all, only shows us a libertine at odds with his victims, who invoke the vengeance of Heaven; while here earth and its dominions try to defeat God. Two nations are here face to face. And Rossini, having every means at his command, has made wonderful use of them. He has succeeded in expressing the turmoil of a tremendous storm as a background to the most terrible imprecations, without making it ridiculous. He has achieved it by the use of chords repeated in triple time - a monotonous rhythm of gloomy musical emphasis - and so persistent as to be quite overpowering. The horror of the Egyptians at the torrent of fire, the cries of vengeance from the Hebrews, needed a delicate balance of masses; so note how he has made the development of the orchestral parts follow that of the chorus. The *allegro assai* in C minor is terrible in the midst of that deluge of fire.

"Confess now," said Massimilla, at the moment when Moses, lifting his rod, brings down the rain of fire, and when the composer puts forth all his powers in the orchestra and on the stage, "that no music ever more perfectly expressed the idea of distress and confusion."

"They have spread to the pit," remarked the Frenchman.

"What is it now? The pit is certainly in great excitement," said the Duchess.

In the *finale*, Genovese, his eyes fixed on la Tinti, had launched into such preposterous flourishes, that the pit, indignant at this interference with their enjoyment, were at a height of uproar. Nothing could be more exasperating to Italian ears than this contrast of good and bad singing. The manager went so far as to appear on the stage, to say that in reply to his remarks to his leading singer, Signor Genovese had replied that he knew not how or by what offence he had lost the countenance of the public, at the very moment when he was endeavoring to achieve perfection in his art.

"Let him be as bad as he was yesterday - that was good enough for us!" roared Capraja, in a rage.

This suggestion put the house into a good humor again.

Contrary to Italian custom, the ballet was not much attended to. In every box the only subject of conversation was Genovese's strange behavior, and the luckless manager's speech. Those who were admitted behind the scenes went off at once to inquire into the mystery of this performance, and it was presently rumored that la Tinti had treated her colleague Genovese to a dreadful scene, in which she had accused the tenor of being jealous of her success, of having hindered it by his ridiculous behavior, and even of trying to spoil her performance by acting passionate devotion. The lady was shedding bitter tears over this catastrophe. She had been hoping, she said, to charm her lover, who was somewhere in the house, though she had failed to discover him.

Without knowing the peaceful course of daily life in Venice at the present day, so devoid of incident that a slight altercation between two lovers, or the transient huskiness of a singer's voice becomes a subject of discussion, regarded of as much importance as politics in England, it is impossible to conceive of the excitement in the theatre and at the Cafe Florian. La Tinti was in love; la Tinti had been hindered in her performance; Genovese was mad or purposely malignant, inspired by the artist's jealousy so familiar to Italians! What a mine of matter for eager discussion!

The whole pit was talking as men talk at the Bourse, and the result was such a clamor as could not fail to amaze a Frenchman accustomed to the quiet of the Paris theatres. The boxes were in a ferment like the stir of swarming bees.

One man alone remained passive in the turmoil. Emilio Memmi, with his back to the stage and his eyes fixed on Massimilla with a melancholy expression, seemed to live in her gaze; he had not once looked round at the prima donna.

"I need not ask you, *caro carino*, what was the result of my negotiation," said Vendramin to Emilio. "Your pure and pious Massimilla has been supremely kind - in short, she has been la Tinti?"

The Prince's reply was a shake of his head, full of the deepest melancholy.

"Your love has not descended from the ethereal spaces

where you soar," said Vendramin, excited by opium. "It is not yet materialized. This morning, as every day for six months - you felt flowers opening their scented cups under the dome of your skull that had expanded to vast proportions. All your blood moved to your swelling heart that rose to choke your throat. There, in there," - and he laid his hand on Emilio's breast, - "you felt rapturous emotions. Massimilla's voice fell on your soul in waves of light; her touch released a thousand imprisoned joys which emerged from the convolutions of your brain to gather about you in clouds, to waft your etherealized body through the blue air to a purple glow far above the snowy heights, to where the pure love of angels dwells. The smile, the kisses of her lips wrapped you in a poisoned robe which burnt up the last vestiges of your earthly nature. Her eyes were twin stars that turned you into shadowless light. You knelt together on the palm-branches of heaven, waiting for the gates of Paradise to be opened; but they turned heavily on their hinges, and in your impatience you struck at them, but could not reach them. Your hand touched nothing but clouds more nimble than your desires. Your radiant companion, crowned with white roses like a bride of Heaven, wept at your anguish. Perhaps she was murmuring melodious litanies to the Virgin, while the demoniacal cravings of the flesh were haunting you with their shameless clamor, and you disdained the divine fruits of that ecstasy in which I live, though shortening my life."

"Your exaltation, my dear Vendramin," replied Emilio, calmly, "is still beneath reality. Who can describe that purely physical exhaustion in which we are left by the abuse of a dream of pleasure, leaving the soul still eternally craving, and the spirit in clear possession of its faculties?

"But I am weary of this torment, which is that of Tantalus. This is my last night on earth. After one final effort, our Mother shall have her child again - the Adriatic will silence my last sigh -"

"Are you idiotic?" cried Vendramin. "No; you are mad; for madness, the crisis we despise, is the memory of an antecedent condition acting on our present state of being. The genius of my dreams has taught me that, and much else! You want to make one of the Duchess and la Tinti; nay, dear Emilio, take them separately; it will be far wiser. Raphael alone ever united form and idea. You want to be the Raphael of love; but chance cannot be commanded. Raphael was a 'fluke' of God's creation, for He foreordained that form and idea should be antagonistic; otherwise nothing could live. When the first cause is more potent than the outcome, nothing comes of it. We must live either on earth or in the skies. Remain in the skies; it is always too soon to come down to earth."

"I will take the Duchess home," said the Prince, "and make a last attempt - afterwards?"

"Afterwards," cried Vendramin, anxiously, "promise to call for me at Florian's."

"I will."

This dialogue, in modern Greek, with which Vendramin and Emilio were familiar, as many Venetians are, was unintelligible to the Duchess and to the Frenchman. Although he was quite outside the little circle that held the Duchess, Emilio and Vendramin together - for these three understood each other by means of Italian glances, by turns arch and keen, or veiled and sidelong - the physician at last discerned part of the truth. An earnest entreaty from the Duchess had prompted Vendramin's suggestion to Emilio, for Massimilla had begun to suspect the misery endured by her lover in that cold empyrean where he was wandering, though she had no suspicions of la Tinti.

"These two young men are mad!" said the doctor.

"As to the Prince," said the Duchess, "trust me to cure him. As to Vendramin, if he cannot understand this sublime music, he is perhaps incurable."

"If you would but tell me the cause of their madness, I could cure them," said the Frenchman.

"And since when have great physicians ceased to read men's minds?" said she, jestingly.

The ballet was long since ended; the second act of *Mose* was beginning. The pit was perfectly attentive. A rumor had got abroad that Duke Cataneo had lectured Genovese, representing to him what injury he was doing to Clarina, the *diva* of the day. The second act would certainly be magnificent.

"The Egyptian Prince and his father are on the stage," said the Duchess. "They have yielded once more, though insulting the Hebrews, but they are trembling with rage. The father congratulates himself on his son's approaching marriage, and the son is in despair at this fresh obstacle, though it only increases his love, to which everything is opposed. Genovese and Cartagenova are singing admirably. As you see, the tenor is making his peace with the house. How well he brings out the beauty of the music! The phrase given out by the son on the tonic, and repeated by the father on the dominant, is all in character with the simple, serious scheme which prevails throughout the score; the sobriety of it makes the endless variety of the music all the more wonderful. All Egypt is there.

"I do not believe that there is in modern music a composition more perfectly noble. The solemn and majestic paternity of a king is fully expressed in that magnificent theme, in harmony with the grand style that stamps the opera throughout. The idea of a Pharaoh's son pouring out his sorrows on his father's bosom could surely not be more admirably represented than in this grand imagery. Do you not feel a sense of the splendor we are wont to attribute to that monarch of antiquity?"

"It is indeed sublime music," said the Frenchman.

"The air *Pace mia smarrita,* which the Queen will now sing, is one of those *bravura* songs which every composer is compelled to introduce, though they mar the general scheme of the work; but an opera would as often as not never see the light, if the prima donna's vanity were not duly flattered. Still, this musical 'sop' is so fine in itself that it is performed as written, on every stage; it is so brilliant that the leading lady does not substitute her favorite show piece, as is very commonly done in operas.

"And now comes the most striking movement in the score: the duet between Osiride and Elcia in the subterranean chamber where he has hidden her to keep her from the departing Israelites, and to fly with her himself from Egypt. The lovers are then intruded on by Aaron, who has been to warn Amalthea, and we get the

Honore de Balzac

grandest of all quartettes: *Mi manca la voce, mi sento morire.* This is one of those masterpieces that will survive in spite of time, that destroyer of fashion in music, for it speaks the language of the soul which can never change. Mozart holds his own by the famous *finale* to *Don Giovanni*; Marcello, by his psalm, *Coeli enarrant gloriam Dei*; Cimarosa, by the air *Pria che spunti*; Beethoven by his C minor symphony; Pergolesi, by his *Stabat Mater*; Rossini will live by *Mi manca la voce.* What is most to be admired in Rossini is his command of variety to form; to produce the effect here required, he has had recourse to the old structure of the canon in unison, to bring the voices in, and merge them in the same melody. As the form of these sublime melodies was new, he set them in an old frame; and to give it the more relief he has silenced the orchestra, accompanying the voices with the harps alone. It is impossible to show greater ingenuity of detail, or to produce a grander general effect. - Dear me! again an outbreak!" said the Duchess.

Genovese, who had sung his duet with Carthagenova so well, was caricaturing himself now that la Tinti was on the stage. From a great singer he sank to the level of the most worthless chorus singer.

The most formidable uproar arose that had ever echoed to the roof of the *Fenice*. The commotion only yielded to Clarina, and she, furious at the difficulties raised by Genovese's obstinacy, sang *Mi manca la voce* as it will never be sung again. The enthusiasm was tremendous; the audience forgot their indignation and rage in pleasure that was really acute.

"She floods my soul with purple glow!" said Capraja, waving his hand in benediction at la *Diva* Tinti.

"Heaven send all its blessings on your head!" cried a gondolier.

"Pharaoh will now revoke his commands," said the Duchess, while the commotion in the pit was calming down. "Moses will overwhelm him, even on his throne, by declaring the death of every first-born son in Egypt, singing that strain of vengeance which augurs thunders from heaven, while above it the Hebrew clarions ring out. But you must clearly understand that this air is by Pacini; Carthagenova introduces it instead of that by Rossini. This air, *Paventa*, will no doubt hold its place in the score; it gives a bass too good an opportunity for displaying the quality of his voice, and expression here will carry the day rather than science. However, the air is full of magnificent menace, and it is possible that we may not be long allowed to hear it."

A thunder of clapping and *bravos* hailed the song, followed by deep and cautious silence; nothing could be more significant or more thoroughly Venetian than the outbreak and its sudden suppression.

"I need say nothing of the coronation march announcing the enthronement of Osiride, intended by the King as a challenge to Moses; to hear it is enough. Their famous Beethoven has written nothing grander. And this march, full of earthly pomp, contrasts finely with the march of the Israelites. Compare them, and you will see that the music is full of purpose.

"Elcia declares her love in the presence of the two Hebrew leaders, and then renounces it in the fine *aria, Porge la destra amata.* (Place your beloved hand.) Ah! What anguish! Only look at the house!"

Honore de Balzac

The pit was shouting *bravo*, when Genovese left the stage.

"Now, free from her deplorable lover, we shall hear Tinti sing, *O desolata Elcia* - the tremendous *cavatina* expressive of love disapproved by God."

"Where art thou, Rossini?" cried Cataneo. "If he could but hear the music created by his genius so magnificently performed," he went on. "Is not Clarina worthy of him?" he asked Capraja. "To give life to those notes by such gusts of flame, starting from the lungs and feeding in the air on some unknown matter which our ears inhale, and which bears us heavenwards in a rapture of love, she must be divine!"

"She is like the gorgeous Indian plant, which deserting the earth absorbs invisible nourishment from the atmosphere, and sheds from its spiral white blossom such fragrant vapors as fill the brain with dreams," replied Capraja.

On being recalled, la Tinti appeared alone. She was received with a storm of applause; a thousand kisses were blown to her from finger-tips; she was pelted with roses, and a wreath was made of the flowers snatched from the ladies' caps, almost all sent out from Paris.

The *cavatina* was encored.

"How eagerly Capraja, with his passion for embellishments, must have looked forward to this air, which derives all its value from execution," remarked Massimilla. "Here Rossini has, so to speak, given the reins over to the singer's fancy. Her *cadenzas* and her feeling are everything. With a poor voice or inferior execution, it would be nothing - the throat is responsible for the effects of this *aria*.

"The singer has to express the most intense anguish, - that of a woman who sees her lover dying before her very eyes. La Tinti makes the house ring with her highest notes; and Rossini, to leave pure singing free to do its utmost, has written it in the simplest, clearest style. Then, as a crowning effort, he has composed those heartrending musical cries: *Tormenti! Affanni! Smanie!* What grief, what anguish, in those runs. And la Tinti, you see, has quite carried the house off its feet."

The Frenchman, bewildered by this adoring admiration throughout a vast theatre for the source of its delight, here had a glimpse of genuine Italian nature. But neither the Duchess nor the two young men paid any attention to the ovation. Clarina began again.

The Duchess feared that she was seeing her Emilio for the last time. As to the Prince: in the presence of the Duchess, the sovereign divinity who lifted him to the skies, he had forgotten where he was, he no longer heard the voice of the woman who had initiated him into the mysteries of earthly pleasure, for deep dejection made his ears tingle with a chorus of plaintive voices, half-drowned in a rushing noise as of pouring rain.

Vendramin saw himself in an ancient Venetian costume, looking on at the ceremony of the *Bucentaur*. The Frenchman, who plainly discerned that some strange and painful mystery stood between the Prince and the Duchess, was racking his brain with shrewd conjecture to discover what it could be.

The scene had changed. In front of a fine picture, representing the Desert and the Red Sea, the Egyptians and Hebrews marched and countermarched without any effect on the feelings of the four persons in the Duchess' box. But when the first chords on the harps preluded the hymn of the delivered Israelites, the Prince and Vendramin rose and stood leaning against the opposite sides of the box, and the Duchess, resting her elbow on the velvet ledge, supported her head on her left hand.

The Frenchman, understanding from this little stir, how important this justly famous chorus was in the opinion of the house, listened with devout attention.

The audience, with one accord, shouted for its repetition.

"I feel as if I were celebrating the liberation of Italy," thought a Milanese.

"Such music lifts up bowed heads, and revives hope in the most torpid," said a man from the Romagna.

"In this scene," said Massimilla, whose emotion was evident, "science is set aside. Inspiration, alone, dictated this masterpiece; it rose from the composer's soul like a cry of love! As to the accompaniment, it consists of the harps; the orchestra appears only at the last repetition of that heavenly strain. Rossini can never rise higher than in this prayer; he will do as good work, no doubt, but never better: the sublime is always equal to itself; but this hymn is one of the things that will always be sublime. The only match for such a conception might be found in the psalms of the great Marcello, a noble Venetian, who was to music what Giotto was to painting. The majesty of the phrase, unfolding itself with episodes of inexhaustible melody, is comparable with the finest things ever invented by religious writers.

"How simple is the structure! Moses opens the attack in G minor, ending in a cadenza in B flat which allows the chorus to come in, *pianissimo* at first, in B flat, returning by modulations to G minor. This splendid treatment of the voices, recurring three times, ends in the last strophe with a *stretto* in G major of absolutely overpowering effect. We feel as though this hymn of a nation released from slavery, as it mounts to heaven, were met by kindred strains falling from the higher spheres. The stars respond with joy to the ecstasy of liberated mortals. The rounded fulness of the rhythm, the deliberate dignity of the graduations leading up to the outbursts of thanksgiving, and its slow return raise heavenly images in the soul. Could you not fancy that you saw heaven open, angels holding sistrums of gold, prostrate seraphs swinging their fragrant censers, and the archangels leaning on the flaming swords with which they have vanquished the heathen?

"The secret of this music and its refreshing effect on the soul is, I believe, that of a very few works of human genius: it carries us for the moment into the infinite; we feel it within us; we see it, in those melodies as boundless as the hymns sung round the throne of God. Rossini's genius carries us up to prodigious heights, whence we look down on a promised land, and our eyes, charmed by heavenly light, gaze into limitless space. Elcia's last strain, having almost recovered from her grief, brings a feeling of earth-born passions into this hymn of thanksgiving. This, again, is a touch of genius.

"Ay, sing!" exclaimed the Duchess, as she listened to the last stanza with the same gloomy enthusiasm as the singers threw into it. "Sing! You are free!"

The words were spoken in a voice that startled the physician. To divert Massimilla from her bitter reflections, while the excitement of recalling la Tinti was at its height, he engaged her in one of the arguments in which the French excel.

"Madame," said he, "in explaining this grand work - which I shall come to hear again to-morrow with a fuller comprehension, thanks to you, of its structure and its effect - you have frequently spoken of the color of the music, and of the ideas it depicts; now I, as an analyst, a materialist, must confess that I have always rebelled against the affectation of certain enthusiasts, who try to make us believe that music paints with tones. Would it not be the same thing if Raphael's admirers spoke of his singing with colors?"

"In the language of musicians," replied the Duchess, "*painting* is arousing certain associations in our souls, or certain images in our brain; and these memories and images have a color of their own; they are sad or cheerful. You are battling for a word, that is all. According to Capraja, each instrument has its task, its mission, and appeals to certain feelings in our souls. Does a pattern in gold on a blue ground produce the same sensations in you as a red pattern on black or green? In these, as in music, there are no figures, no expression of feeling; they are purely artistic, and yet no one looks at them with indifference. Has not the oboe the peculiar tone that we associate with the open country, in common with most wind instruments? The brass suggests martial ideas, and rouses us to vehement or even somewhat furious feelings. The strings, for which the material is derived from the organic world, seem to appeal to the subtlest fibres of our nature; they go to the very depths of the heart. When I spoke of the gloomy hue, and the coldness of the tones in the introduction to *Mose*, was I not fully as much justified as your critics are when they speak of the 'color' in a writer's language? Do you not acknowledge that there is a nervous style, a pallid style, a lively, and a highly-colored style? Art can paint with words, sounds, colors, lines, form; the means are many; the result is one.

"An Italian architect might give us the same sensation that is produced in us by the introduction to *Mose*, by constructing a walk through dark, damp avenues of tall, thick trees, and bringing us out suddenly in a valley full of streams, flowers, and mills, and basking in the sunshine. In their greatest moments the arts are but the expression of the grand scenes of nature.

"I am not learned enough to enlarge on the philosophy of music; go and talk to Capraja; you will be amazed at what he can tell you. He will say that every instrument that depends on the touch or breath of man for its expression and length of note, is superior as a vehicle of expression to color, which remains fixed, or speech, which has its limits. The language of music is infinite; it includes everything; it can express all things.

"Now do you see wherein lies the pre-eminence of the work you have just heard? I can explain it in a few words. There are two kinds of music: one, petty, poor, second-rate, always the same, based on a hundred or so of phrases which every musician has at his command, a more or less agreeable form of babble which most composers live in. We listen to their strains, their would-be melodies, with more or less satisfaction, but absolutely nothing is left in our mind; by the end of the century they are forgotten. But the nations, from the beginning of time till our own day, have cherished as a precious treasure certain strains which epitomize their instincts and habits; I might almost say their history. Listen to one of these primitive tones, - the Gregorian chant, for instance, is, in sacred song, the inheritance of the earliest peoples, - and you will lose yourself in deep dreaming. Strange and immense conceptions will unfold within you, in spite of the extreme simplicity of these rudimentary relics. And once or twice in a century - not oftener, there arises a Homer of music, to whom God grants the gift of being ahead of his age; men who can compact melodies full of accomplished facts, pregnant with mighty poetry. Think of this; remember it. The thought, repeated by you, will prove fruitful; it is melody, not harmony, that can survive the shocks of time.

"The music of this oratorio contains a whole world of great and sacred things. A work which begins with that introduction and ends with that prayer is immortal - as immortal as the Easter hymn, *O filii et filioe*, as the *Dies iroe* of the dead, as all the songs which in every land have outlived its splendor, its happiness, and its ruined prosperity."

The tears the Duchess wiped away as she quitted her box showed plainly that she was thinking of the Venice that is no more; and Vendramin kissed her hand.

The performance ended with the most extraordinary chaos of noises: abuse and hisses hurled at Genovese and a fit of frenzy in praise of la Tinti. It was a long time since the Venetians had had so lively an evening. They were warmed and revived by that antagonism which is never lacking in Italy, where the smallest towns always throve on the antagonistic interests of two factions: the Geulphs and Ghibellines everywhere; the Capulets and the Montagues at Verona; the Geremei and the Lomelli at Bologna; the Fieschi and the Doria at Genoa; the patricians and the populace, the Senate and tribunes of the Roman republic; the Pazzi and the Medici at Florence; the Sforza and the Visconti at Milan; the Orsini and the Colonna at Rome, - in short, everywhere and on every occasion there has been the same impulse.

Out in the streets there were already *Genovists* and *Tintists*.

The Prince escorted the Duchess, more depressed than ever by the loves of Osiride; she feared some similar disaster to her own, and could only cling to Emilio, as if to keep him next her heart.

"Remember your promise," said Vendramin. "I will wait for you in the square."

Vendramin took the Frenchman's arm, proposing that they should walk together on the Piazza San Marco while awaiting the Prince.

"I shall be only too glad if he should not come," he added.

This was the text for a conversation between the two,

Honore de Balzac

Vendramin regarding it as a favorable opportunity for consulting the physician, and telling him the singular position Emilio had placed himself in.

The Frenchman did as every Frenchman does on all occasions: he laughed. Vendramin, who took the matter very seriously, was angry; but he was mollified when the disciple of Majendie, of Cuvier, of Dupuytren, and of Brossais assured him that he believed he could cure the Prince of his high-flown raptures, and dispel the heavenly poetry in which he shrouded Massimilla as in a cloud.

"A happy form of misfortune!" said he. "The ancients, who were not such fools as might be inferred from their crystal heaven and their ideas on physics, symbolized in the fable of Ixion the power which nullifies the body and makes the spirit lord of all."

Vendramin and the doctor presently met Genovese, and with him the fantastic Capraja. The melomaniac was anxious to learn the real cause of the tenor's *fiasco*. Genovese, the question being put to him, talked fast, like all men who can intoxicate themselves by the ebullition of ideas suggested to them by a passion.

"Yes, signori, I love her, I worship her with a frenzy of which I never believed myself capable, now that I am tired of women. Women play the mischief with art. Pleasure and work cannot be carried on together. Clara fancies that I was jealous of her success, that I wanted to hinder her triumph at Venice; but I was clapping in the side-scenes, and shouted *Diva* louder than any one in the house."

"But even that," said Cataneo, joining them, "does not

explain why, from being a divine singer, you should have become one of the most execrable performers who ever piped air through his larynx, giving none of the charm even which enchants and bewitches us."

"I!" said the singer. "I a bad singer! I who am the equal of the greatest performers!"

By this time, the doctor and Vendramin, Capraja, Cataneo, and Genovese had made their way to the piazzetta. It was midnight. The glittering bay, outlined by the churches of San Giorgio and San Paulo at the end of the Giudecca, and the beginning of the Grand Canal, that opens so mysteriously under the *Dogana* and the church of Santa Maria della Salute, lay glorious and still. The moon shone on the barques along the Riva de' Schiavoni. The waters of Venice, where there is no tide, looked as if they were alive, dancing with a myriad spangles. Never had a singer a more splendid stage.

Genovese, with an emphatic flourish, seemed to call Heaven and Earth to witness; and then, with no accompaniment but the lapping waves, he sang *Ombra adorata*, Crescentini's great air. The song, rising up between the statues of San Teodoro and San Giorgio, in the heart of sleeping Venice lighted by the moon, the words, in such strange harmony with the scene, and the melancholy passion of the singer, held the Italians and the Frenchman spellbound.

At the very first notes, Vendramin's face was wet with tears. Capraja stood as motionless as one of the statues in the ducal palace. Cataneo seemed moved to some feeling. The Frenchman, taken by surprise, was meditative, like a man of science in the presence of a phenomenon that upsets all his fundamental axioms. These four minds, all so different, whose hopes were so small, who believed in nothing for themselves or after themselves, who regarded their own existence as that of a transient and a fortuitous being, - like the little life of a plant or a beetle, - had a glimpse of Heaven. Never did music more truly merit the epithet divine. The consoling notes, as they were poured out, enveloped their souls in soft and soothing airs. On these vapors, almost visible, as it seemed to the listeners, like the marble shapes about them in the silver moonlight, angels sat whose wings, devoutly waving, expressed adoration and love. The simple, artless melody penetrated to the soul as with a beam of light. It was a holy passion!

But the singer's vanity roused them from their emotion with a terrible shock.

"Now, am I a bad singer?" he exclaimed, as he ended.

His audience only regretted that the instrument was not a thing of Heaven. This angelic song was then no more than the outcome of a man's offended vanity! The singer felt nothing, thought nothing, of the pious sentiments and divine images he could create in others, - no more, in fact, than Paganini's violin knows what the player makes it utter. What they had seen in fancy was Venice lifting its shroud and singing - and it was merely the result of a tenor's *fiasco*!

"Can you guess the meaning of such a phenomenon?" the Frenchman asked of Capraja, wishing to make him talk, as the Duchess had spoken of him as a profound thinker.

"What phenomenon?" said Capraja.

"Genovese - who is admirable in the absence of la Tinti, and when he sings with her is a braying ass."

"He obeys an occult law of which one of your chemists might perhaps give you the mathematical formula, and which the next century will no doubt express in a statement full of x, a, and b, mixed up with little algebraic signs, bars, and quirks that give me the colic; for the finest conceptions of mathematics do not add much to the sum total of our enjoyment.

"When an artist is so unfortunate as to be full of the passion he wishes to express, he cannot depict it because he is the thing itself instead of its image. Art is the work of the brain, not of the heart. When you are possessed by a subject you are a slave, not a master; you are like a king besieged by his people. Too keen a feeling, at the moment when you want to represent that feeling, causes an insurrection of the senses against the governing faculty."

"Might we not convince ourselves of this by some further experiment?" said the doctor.

"Cataneo, you might bring your tenor and the prima donna together again," said Capraja to his friend.

"Well, gentlemen," said the Duke, "come to sup with me. We ought to reconcile the tenor and la Clarina; otherwise the season will be ruined in Venice."

The invitation was accepted.

"Gondoliers!" called Cataneo.

"One minute," said Vendramin. "Memmi is waiting for me at Florian's; I cannot leave him to himself. We must make him tipsy to-night, or he will kill himself to-morrow."

"*Corpo santo!*" exclaimed the Duke. "I must keep that young fellow alive, for the happiness and future prospects of my race. I will invite him, too."

They all went back to Florian's, where the assembled crowd were holding an eager and stormy discussion to which the tenor's arrival put an end. In one corner, near a window looking out on the colonnade, gloomy, with a fixed gaze and rigid attitude, Emilio was a dismal image of despair.

"That crazy fellow," said the physician, in French, to Vendramin, "does not know what he wants. Here is a man who can make of a Massimilla Doni a being apart from the rest of creation, possessing her in heaven, amid ideal splendor such as no power on earth can make real. He can behold his mistress for ever sublime and pure, can always hear within him what we have just heard on the seashore; can always live in the light of a pair of eyes which create for him the warm and golden glow that surrounds the Virgin in Titian's Assumption, - after Raphael had invented it or had it revealed to him for the Transfiguration, - and this man only longs to smirch the poem.

"By my advice he must needs combine his sensual joys and his heavenly adoration in one woman. In short, like all the rest of us, he will have a mistress. He had a divinity, and the wretched creature insists on her being a female! I assure you, monsieur, he is resigning heaven. I will not answer for it that he may not ultimately die of despair.

"O ye women's faces, delicately outlined in a pure and radiant oval, reminding us of those creations of art where it has most successfully competed with nature! Divine feet that cannot walk, slender forms that an earthly breeze would break, shapes too frail ever to conceive, virgins that we dreamed of as we grew out of childhood, admired in secret, and adored without hope, veiled in the beams of some unwearying desire, - maids whom we may never see again, but whose smile remains supreme in our life, what hog of Epicurus could insist on dragging you down to the mire of this earth!

"The sun, monsieur, gives light and heat to the world, only because it is at a distance of thirty-three millions of leagues. Get nearer to it, and science warns you that it is not really hot or luminous, - for science is of some use," he added, looking at Capraja.

"Not so bad for a Frenchman and a doctor," said Capraja, patting the foreigner on the shoulder. "You have in those words explained the thing which Europeans least understand in all Dante: his Beatrice. Yes, Beatrice, that ideal figure, the queen of the poet's fancies, chosen above all the elect, consecrated with tears, deified by memory, and for ever young in the presence of ineffectual desire!"

"Prince," said the Duke to Emilio, "come and sup with me. You cannot refuse the poor Neapolitan whom you have robbed both of his wife and of his mistress."

This broad Neapolitan jest, spoken with an aristocratic good manner, made Emilio smile; he allowed the Duke to take his arm and lead him away.

Cataneo had already sent a messenger to his house from the cafe.

As the Palazzo Memmi was on the Grand Canal, not far from Santa Maria della Salute, the way thither on foot was round by the Rialto, or it could be reached in a gondola. The four guests would not separate and preferred to walk; the Duke's infirmities obliged him to get into his gondola.

At about two in the morning anybody passing the Memmi palace would have seen light pouring out of every window across the Grand Canal, and have heard the delightful overture to *Semiramide* performed at the foot of the steps by the orchestra of the *Fenice*, as a serenade to la Tinti.

The company were at supper in the second floor gallery. From the balcony la Tinti in return sang Almavida's *Buona sera* from *Il Barbiere*, while the Duke's steward distributed payment from his master to the poor artists and bid them to dinner the next day, such civilities as are expected of grand signors who protect singers, and of fine ladies who protect tenors and basses. In these cases there is nothing for it but to marry all the *corps de theatre*.

Cataneo did things handsomely; he was the manager's banker, and this season was costing him two thousand crowns.

He had had all the palace furnished, had imported a French cook, and wines of all lands. So the supper was a regal entertainment.

The Prince, seated next la Tinti, was keenly alive, all through the meal, to what poets in every language call the darts of love. The transcendental vision of Massimilla was eclipsed, just as the idea of God is sometimes hidden by clouds of doubt in the consciousness of solitary thinkers. Clarina thought herself the happiest woman in the world as she perceived Emilio was in love with her. Confident of retaining him, her joy was reflected in her features, her beauty was so dazzling that the men, as they lifted their glasses, could not resist bowing to her with instinctive admiration.

"The Duchess is not to compare with la Tinti," said the Frenchman, forgetting his theory under the fire of the Sicilian's eyes.

The tenor ate and drank languidly; he seemed to care only to identify himself with the prima donna's life, and had lost the hearty sense of enjoyment which is characteristic of Italian men singers.

"Come, signorina," said the Duke, with an imploring glance at Clarina, "and you, *caro prima uomo*," he added to Genovese, "unite your voices in one perfect sound. Let us have the C of *Qual portento*, when light appears in the oratorio we have just heard, to convince my old friend Capraja of the superiority of unison to any embellishment."

"I will carry her off from that Prince she is in love with; for she adores him - it stares me in the face!" said Genovese to himself.

What was the amazement of the guests who had heard Genovese out of doors, when he began to bray, to coo, mew, squeal, gargle, bellow, thunder, bark, shriek, even produce sounds which could only be described as a hoarse rattle, - in short, go through an incomprehensible farce, while his face was transfigured with rapturous expression like that of a martyr, as painted by Zurbaran or Murillo, Titian or Raphael. The general shout of laughter changed to almost tragical gravity when they saw that Genovese was in utter earnest. La Tinti understood that her companion was in love with her, and had spoken the truth on the stage, the land of falsehood.

"*Poverino!*" she murmured, stroking the Prince's hand under the table.

"By all that is holy!" cried Capraja, "will you tell me what score you are reading at this moment - murdering Rossini? Pray inform us what you are thinking about, what demon is struggling in your throat."

"A demon!" cried Genovese, "say rather the god of music. My eyes, like those of Saint-Cecilia, can see angels, who, pointing with their fingers, guide me along the lines of the score which is written in notes of fire, and I am trying to keep up with them. PER DIO! do you not understand? The feeling that inspires me has passed into my being; it fills my heart and my lungs; my soul and throat have but one life.

"Have you never, in a dream, listened to the most glorious strains, the ideas of unknown composers who have made use of pure sound as nature has hidden it in all things, - sound which we call forth, more or less perfectly, by the instruments we employ to produce masses of various color; but which in those dream-concerts are heard free from the imperfections of the performers who cannot be all feeling, all soul? And I, I give you that perfection, and you abuse me!

"You are as mad at the pit of the *Fenice*, who hissed me! I scorned the vulgar crowd for not being able to mount with me to the heights whence we reign over art, and I appeal to men of mark, to a Frenchman - Why, he is gone!"

"Half an hour ago," said Vendramin.

"That is a pity. He, perhaps, would have understood me, since Italians, lovers of art, do not -"

"On you go!" said Capraja, with a smile, and tapping lightly on the tenor's head. "Ride off on the divine Ariosto's hippogriff; hunt down your radiant chimera, musical visionary as you are!"

In point of fact, all the others, believing that Genovese was drunk, let him talk without listening to him. Capraja alone had understood the case put by the French physician.

While the wine of Cyprus was loosening every tongue, and each one was prancing on his favorite hobby, the doctor, in a gondola, was waiting for the Duchess, having sent her a note written by Vendramin. Massimilla appeared in her night wrapper, so much had she been alarmed by the tone of the Prince's farewell, and so startled by the hopes held out by the letter.

"Madame," said the Frenchman, as he placed her in a seat and desired the gondoliers to start, "at this moment Prince Emilio's life is in danger, and you alone can save him."

"What is to be done?" she asked.

"Ah! Can you resign yourself to play a degrading part - in spite of the noblest face to be seen in Italy? Can you drop from the blue sky where you dwell, into the bed of a courtesan? In short, can you, an angel of refinement, of pure and spotless beauty, condescend to imagine what the love must be of a Tinti - in her room, and so effectually as to deceive the ardor of Emilio, who is indeed too drunk to be very clear-sighted?"

"Is that all?" said she, with a smile that betrayed to the Frenchman a side he had not as yet perceived of the delightful nature of an Italian woman in love. "I will out-do la Tinti, if need be, to save my friend's life."

"And you will thus fuse into one two kinds of love, which he sees as distinct - divided by a mountain of poetic fancy, that will melt away like the snow on a glacier under the beams of the midsummer sun."

"I shall be eternally your debtor," said the Duchess, gravely.

When the French doctor returned to the gallery, where the orgy had by this time assumed the stamp of Venetian frenzy, he had a look of satisfaction which the Prince, absorbed by la Tinti, failed to observe; he was promising himself a repetition of the intoxicating delights he had known. La Tinti, a true Sicilian, was floating on the tide of a fantastic passion on the point of being gratified.

The doctor whispered a few words to Vendramin, and la Tinti was uneasy.

"What are you plotting?" she inquired of the Prince's friend.

"Are you kind-hearted?" said the doctor in her ear, with the sternness of an operator.

The words pierced to her comprehension like a dagger-thrust to her heart.

"It is to save Emilio's life," added Vendramin.

"Come here," said the doctor to Clarina.

The hapless singer rose and went to the other end of the table where, between Vendramin and the Frenchman, she looked like a criminal between the confessor and the executioner.

She struggled for a long time, but yielded at last for love of Emilio.

The doctor's last words were:

"And you must cure Genovese!"

She spoke a word to the tenor as she went round the table. She returned to the Prince, put her arm round his neck and kissed his hair with an expression of despair which struck Vendramin and the Frenchman, the only two who had their wits about them, then she vanished into her room. Emilio, seeing Genovese leave the table, while Cataneo and Capraja were absorbed in a long musical discussion, stole to the door of the bedroom, lifted the curtain, and slipped in, like an eel into the mud.

"But you see, Cataneo," said Capraja, "you have exacted the last drop of physical enjoyment, and there you are, hanging on a wire like a cardboard harlequin, patterned with scars, and never moving unless the string is pulled of a perfect unison."

"And you, Capraja, who have squeezed ideas dry, are not you in the same predicament? Do you not live riding the hobby of a *cadenza*?"

"I? I possess the whole world!" cried Capraja, with a sovereign gesture of his hand.

"And I have devoured it!" replied the Duke.

They observed that the physician and Vendramin were gone, and that they were alone.

Next morning, after a night of perfect happiness, the Prince's sleep was disturbed by a dream. He felt on his heart the trickle of pearls, dropped there by an angel; he woke, and found himself bathed in the tears of Massimilla Doni. He was lying in her arms, and she gazed at him as he slept.

That evening, at the *Fenice*, - though la Tinti had not allowed him to rise till two in the afternoon, which is said to be very bad for a tenor voice, - Genovese sang divinely in his part in *Semiramide*. He was recalled with la Tinti, fresh crowns were given, the pit was wild with delight; the tenor no longer attempted to charm the prima donna by angelic methods.

Vendramin was the only person whom the doctor could not cure. Love for a country that has ceased to be is a love beyond curing. The young Venetian, by dint of living in his thirteenth century republic, and in the arms of that pernicious courtesan called opium, when he found himself in the work-a-day world to which reaction brought him, succumbed, pitied and regretted by his friends.

No, how shall the end of this adventure be told - for it is too disastrously domestic. A word will be enough for the worshipers of the ideal.

The Duchess was expecting an infant.

The Peris, the naiads, the fairies, the sylphs of ancient legend, the Muses of Greece, the Marble Virgins of the Certosa at Pavia, the Day and Night of Michael Angelo, the little Angels which Bellini was the first to put at the foot of his Church pictures, and which Raphael painted so divinely in his Virgin with the Donor, and the Madonna who shivers at Dresden, the lovely Maidens by Orcagna in the Church of San-Michele, at Florence, the celestial choir round the tomb in Saint-Sebaldus, at Nuremberg, the Virgins of the Duomo, at Milan, the whole population of a hundred Gothic Cathedrals, all the race of beings who burst their mould to visit you, great imaginative artists - all these angelic and disembodied maidens gathered round Massimilla's bed, and wept!

PARIS, May 25th, 1839.

Honore de Balzac

Choose from Thousands of 1stWorldLibrary Classics By

Adolphus WilliamWard
Aesop
Agatha Christie
Alexander Aaronsohn
Alexander Kielland
Alexandre Dumas
Alfred Gatty
Alfred Ollivant
Alice Duer Miller
Alice Turner Curtis
Alice Dunbar
Ambrose Bierce
Amelia E. Barr
Andrew Lang
Andrew McFarland Davis
Anna Sewell
Annie Besant
Annie Hamilton Donnell
Annie Payson Call
Anton Chekhov
Arnold Bennett
Arthur Conan Doyle
Arthur Ransome
Atticus
B. M. Bower
Basil King
Bayard Taylor
Ben Macomber
Booth Tarkington
Bram Stoker
C. Collodi
C. E. Orr
C. M. Ingleby
Carolyn Wells
Catherine Parr Traill
Charles A. Eastman
Charles Dickens
Charles Dudley Warner
Charles Farrar Browne
Charles Ives
Charles Kingsley
Charles Lathrop Pack
Charles Whibley
Charles Willing Beale
Charlotte M. Braeme
Charlotte M.Yonge
Clair W. Hayes
Clarence Day Jr.
Clarence E. Mulford

Clemence Housman
Confucius
Cornelis DeWitt Wilcox
Cyril Burleigh
D. H. Lawrence
Daniel Defoe
David Garnett
Don Carlos Janes
Donald Keyhole
Dorothy Kilner
Dougan Clark
E. Nesbit
E.P.Roe
E. Phillips Oppenheim
Edgar Allan Poe
Edgar Rice Burroughs
Edith Wharton
Edward J. O'Biren
John Cournos
Edwin L. Arnold
Eleanor Atkins
Elizabeth Cleghorn
Gaskell
Elizabeth Von Arnim
Ellem Key
Emily Dickinson
Erasmus W. Jones
Ernie Howard Pie
Ethel Turner
Ethel Watts Mumford
Eugenie Foa
Eugene Wood
Evelyn Everett-Green
Everard Cotes
F. J. Cross
Federick Austin Ogg
Ferdinand Ossendowski
Francis Bacon
Francis Darwin
Frances Hodgson Burnett
Frank Gee Patchin
Frank Harris
Frank Jewett Mather
Frank L. Packard
Frederick Trevor Hill
Frederick Winslow Taylor
Friedrich Kerst
Friedrich Nietzsche
Fyodor Dostoyevsky

Gabrielle E. Jackson
Garrett P. Serviss
Gaston Leroux
George Ade
Geroge Bernard Shaw
George Ebers
George Eliot
George MacDonald
George Orwell
George Tucker
George W. Cable
George Wharton James
Gertrude Atherton
Grace E. King
Grant Allen
Guillermo A. Sherwell
Gulielma Zollinger
Gustav Flaubert
H. A. Cody
H. B. Irving
H. G. Wells
H. H. Munro
H. Irving Hancock
H. Rider Haggard
H. W. C. Davis
Hamilton Wright Mabie
Hans Christian Andersen
Harold Avery
Harold McGrath
Harriet Beecher Stowe
Harry Houidini
Helent Hunt Jackson
Helen Nicolay
Hendy David Thoreau
Henrik Ibsen
Henry Adams
Henry Ford
Henry Frost
Henry James
Henry Jones Ford
Henry Seton Merriman
Henry Wadsworth
Longfellow
Henry W Longfellow
Herbert A. Giles
Herbert N. Casson
Herman Hesse
Homer
Honore De Balzac

Horace Walpole
Horatio Alger, Jr.
Howard Pyle
Howard R. Garis
Hugh Lofting
Hugh Walpole
Humphry Ward
Ian Maclaren
Israel Abrahams
J.G.Austin
J. Henri Fabre
J. M. Barrie
J. Macdonald Oxley
J. S. Knowles
J. Storer Clouston
Jack London
Jacob Abbott
James Allen
James Lane Allen
James Andrews
James Baldwin
James DeMille
James Joyce
James Oliver Curwood
James Oppenheim
James Otis
Jane Austen
Jens Peter Jacobsen
Jerome K. Jerome
John Burroughs
John F. Kennedy
John Gay
John Glasworthy
John Habberton
John Joy Bell
John Milton
John Philip Sousa
Jonathan Swift
Joseph Carey
Joseph Conrad
Joseph Jacobs
Julian Hawthrone
Julies Vernes
Justin Huntly McCarthy
Kakuzo Okakura
Kenneth Grahame
Kate Langley Bosher
L. A. Abbot
L. T. Meade
L. Frank Baum
Laura Lee Hope

Laurence Housman
Leo Tolstoy
Leonid Andreyev
Lewis Carroll
Lilian Bell
Lloyd Osbourne
Louis Tracy
Louisa May Alcott
Lucy Fitch Perkins
Lucy Maud Montgomery
Lydia Miller Middleton
Lyndon Orr
M. H. Adams
Margaret E. Sangster
Margaret Vandercook
Maria Edgeworth
Maria Thompson Daviess
Mariano Azuela
Marion Polk Angellotti
Mark Overton
Mark Twain
Mary Austin
Mary Cole
Mary Rowlandson
Mary Wollstonecraft
Shelley
Max Beerbohm
Myra Kelly
Nathaniel Hawthrone
O. F. Walton
Oscar Wilde
Owen Johnson
P.G.Wodehouse
Paul and Mable Thorn
Paul G. Tomlinson
Paul Severing
Peter B. Kyne
Plato
R. Derby Holmes
R. L. Stevenson
Rabindranath Tagore
Rahul Alvares
Ralph Waldo Emmerson
Rene Descartes
Rex E. Beach
Richard Harding Davis
Richard Jefferies
Robert Barr
Robert Frost
Robert Gordon Anderson
Robert L. Drake

Robert Lansing
Robert Michael Ballantyne
Robert W. Chambers
Rosa Nouchette Carey
Ross Kay
Rudyard Kipling
Samuel B. Allison
Samuel Hopkins Adams
Sarah Bernhardt
Selma Lagerlof
Sherwood Anderson
Sigmund Freud
Standish O'Grady
Stanley Weyman
Stella Benson
Stephen Crane
Stewart Edward White
Stijn Streuvels
Swami Abhedananda
Swami Parmananda
T. S. Ackland
The Princess Der Ling
Thomas A. Janvier
Thomas A Kempis
Thomas Anderton
Thomas Bailey Aldrich
Thomas Bulfinch
Thomas De Quincey
Thomas H. Huxley
Thomas Hardy
Thomas More
Thornton W. Burgess
U. S. Grant
Valentine Williams
Victor Appleton
Virginia Woolf
Walter Scott
Washington Irving
Wilbur Lawton
Wilkie Collins
Willa Cather
Willard F. Baker
William Makepeace
Thackeray
William W. Walter
Winston Churchill
Yei Theodora Ozaki
Young E. Allison
Zane Grey

www.ingramcontent.com/pod-product-compliance
Lightning Source LLC
Chambersburg PA
CBHW031841170626
46807CB00004B/1565